MARCUS AURELIUS BETRAYED

A JUDGE MARCUS FLAVIUS SEVERUS MYSTERY IN ANCIENT ROME

ALAN SCRIBNER

MARCUS AURELIUS
BETRAYED

A JUDGE MARCUS FLAVIUS SEVERUS
MYSTERY IN ANCIENT ROME

ALAN SCRIBNER

Torcular Press

ISBN: 1500522856
ISBN 13: 9781500522858
Library of Congress Control Number: 2014912807
CreateSpace Independent Publishing Platform
North Charleston, South Carolina

Dedication
Ruth and Paul

TABLE OF CONTENTS

EPILOGUE

PERSONAE

Marcus Flavius Severus - Judge in the Court of the Urban Prefect of Rome and special Imperial emissary

Judge Severus' *familia* and court staff
Artemisia - Severus' wife
Aulus, Flavia and Quintus, their 12, 10, and 4-year old children
Alexander - freedman and private secretary
Quintus Proculus - court clerk
Caius Vulso - Centurion in the Urban Cohort
Publius Aelianus Straton - Tesserarius in the Urban Cohort
Gaius Sempronius Flaccus - judicial assessor
Glycon – slave
Galatea – slave
Argos – family dog
Phaon – family cat

People in Rome
Marcus Aurelius – Roman Emperor
Quintus Junius Rusticus – Prefect of the City of Rome
Publius Cornelius Naso – Tribune of the Praetorian Guard

Titus Velleius – Praetorian guardsman
Claudius Celer – formerly assistant to Titus Pudens at the Imperial Post in Alexandria
Aulus Gellius – friend of Severus from student days in Athens
Favorinus – famous scholar

People in Alexandria
Marcus Annius Calvus - Prefect of Egypt
Secundus - The Prefect's stepson and personal aide
Titus Pudens – official at the Imperial Post in Alexandria
Philogenes - Homeric scholar and librarian at the Great Library of Alexandria
Petamon - a priest of Isis
Isarion - antique dealer from Alexandria
Serpentinus – aide to the Prefect of Egypt
Ganymede - slave of the Prefect
Rufus – *quaestionarius*
Selene - proprietress of the House of Selene
Hetairai in the House of Selene and present at the Prefect's orgy:
    Zoe, Aurora, Pulcheria, Demetria, Chloe, Eudoxia, Andromache
Cupid – friend of Secundus
Psen-Mon – acolyte-priest of Isis
Manassah ben Jacob – Jewish scholar
Archelaus – official at the Imperial Post

Others
Tiberius Valens – Trierarch of the warship *Argo*
Septimus Eggius – Secundus' lawyer
Avidius Cassius - Roman General on the Persian front

The story is set in Rome and Alexandria in the Roman province of Egypt in the year 163 CE during the reign of the co-Emperors Marcus Aurelius and Lucius Verus. This is two years after the events in *The Cyclops Case* and five years after the events in *Mars the Avenger*.

Times of day: The Roman day was divided into 12 day hours, starting from sunrise and 12 night hours from sunset. The length of the hour and the onset time of the hour depended on the season since there is more daylight in summer, more night in winter.

In the Spring and Fall, close to an equinox, the hours were approximately equal to ours in length and the times of day mentioned in the book are as follows:

1st hour of the day = 6-7 am
2nd hour of the day = 7-8 am
3rd hour of the day = 8-9 am
4th hour of the day = 9-10 am
5th hour of the day = 10-11 am
8th hour of the day = 1-2 pm
9th hour of the day = 2-3 pm
2nd hour of the night = 7-8 pm
4th hour of the night = 9-10 pm

Bust of Marcus Aurelius in about
163 CE at the age of 42

ANCIENT ALEXANDRIA

Above: Looking west along the Canopic Way toward
the Moon Gate
Below: Pharos Lighthouse

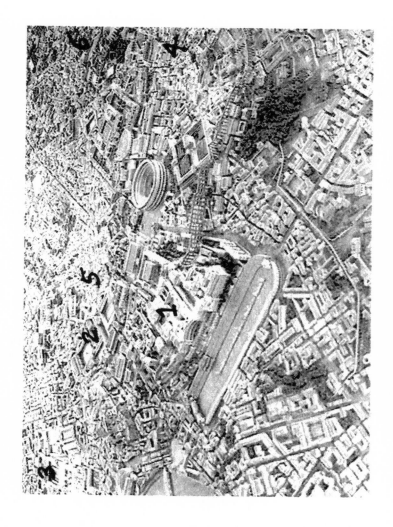

ANCIENT ROME

The picture on the left shows part of the model of ancient Rome in the Museum of Roman Civilization in Rome.

The numbers on the picture locate places mentioned in the book, according to the following key:

1. The Palatine Hill and imperial palace complex

2. The Forum of Augustus, where Severus has his courtroom and chambers

3. The Saepta Julia marketplace

4. The Caelian Hill area, where Severus lives and where he and Marcus Aurelius grew up.

5. The Subura

6. The Esquiline Hill area

SCROLL I

SEVERUS IN EGYPT

MARCUS FLAVIUS SEVERUS
TO HIMSELF

Our Emperor Marcus Aurelius once said to me, "life is warfare and a brief sojourn in an alien land." I think of that often because I've often felt its truth, that traversing life requires warring and soldiering, no matter what station you find yourself in. Regardless of appearances, emperors and slaves, and everyone in between, have to struggle in life one way or another. Not all the time, but inevitably. And Aurelius' Stoic philosophy was as necessary for him in that struggle as it was for the crippled slave Epictetus whose Stoic teachings Aurelius admired so much. For we all find ourselves born into a strange place where we live for a very short time. "The whole Earth is but a point in the cosmos," Aurelius says, "and our lives a point between the vast eons before us and the endless time after us."

I got to know the Emperor personally when, upon the recommendation of his friend and teacher, the Urban Prefect Quintus Junius Rusticus, he appointed me an imperial emissary to Egypt and a *iudex selectus*, a special judge, to discover who tried to assassinate the Prefect of Egypt. On the one hand, that investigation involved me in murder, crime and corruption, on the other it drew me into the world of Marcus Aurelius in a deep way and gained for me an association with a great, though troubled, soul. He was a soul who inevitably was betrayed because his ideals, his vision and his way of life did not conform to the world's; they were not really compatible. As one example, he told me he hated the gladiatorial games, yet he had to attend. No one else in Rome had to go, if he chose not to. But Aurelius, the philosopher, the Emperor, was required to attend, lest he endanger his reign. Yes, he could read and sign documents during the Games and not pay much attention, but he had to be there. He once tried to introduce gladiatorial combats with wooden swords, but the spectators wouldn't have it. So he had to see the blood, the pain, the death, and he had to hear the roar of the crowd, the thousands of his fellow men and women who loved it and for whom it was a major part of their emotional lives. But for Aurelius, it was a personal war to get himself to attend and preside at the amphitheater, an arena of death alien to his philosophy of life.

I was brought to meet him by the Urban Prefect in order to receive an imperial appointment. But this was not the first time I had met Marcus Aurelius. As children we lived in the same neighborhood on the Caelian Hill, he in his parents' wealthy city *domus* town house, me in my parents' luxury *insula* apartment house. We occasionally played together on the street with the other 'chicks'. But that was years before the Emperor Hadrian picked him out to be adopted into the imperial family and trained for future greatness. When I knew him he was just a 'chick' like the rest of us.

I wondered when I was brought to see him on the Palatine if he might remember me from our childhood.

I

AN AUDIENCE WITH THE EMPEROR

Marcus Flavius Severus, judge in the Court of the Urban Prefect, was escorted to the Palatine Hill by the Urban Prefect, Quintus Junius Rusticus. They both wore freshly laundered spotless white togas with the reddish-purple border of judicial authority. Rusticus' tunic showing through the gap in the toga bore the broad reddish-purple stripe of a member of the Senatorial Order, while Severus' tunic stripes were the same color, but he wore the narrow stripe of the Equestrian Order. At the second hour of the morning, under a resplendent and warming sun, they ascended to the Palatine in litters from the Old Forum up the Clivus Victoriae, the slope of victory, and were carried toward the *Aula Regia*, the royal hall and the throne room.

The Palatine was already a busy place. Swarms of officials darted in and out of buildings, conferred on the streets, in the porticoes, on the steps of palaces and administrative buildings. The Palatine was not just the residence of the Emperor and the imperial family, but the center of a large and complex government. There were the major government Bureaus, among them Treasury, Judicial Affairs, Latin and Greek Correspondence and the Bureau of Petitions. It was the seat of deals and negotiations and policy assessments and the place where hopes and dreams were every day encouraged, frustrated, fulfilled, crushed, delayed. The buildings were beautiful, with marbled columns, intricate mosaics and sculptured pediments, set amidst gardens and libraries and awnings of every color, though on the Palatine purple awnings were the favored color.

The litters were carried behind the House of Augustus to the *Aula Regia*, built by the Emperor Domitian 75 years before. Severus and Rusticus were helped out of their litters by waiting slaves who made certain their judicial togas did not touch the ground. They were then escorted into the vestibule. There, they had to wait with others waiting to see the Emperor to pay respects, to seek favors, to transact business. Among those waiting there were animated discussions and nervous silences. Some looked ethereal, some tried to appear nonchalant and some looked sick. One of those waiting, Severus noticed, was the famous hermaphrodite and albino sage and scholar Favorinus. He was surrounded by others who seemed to be enjoying him putting down an arrogant and pretentious poseur with a remarkable display of literary erudition. But Severus was himself a little too nervous to pay attention to the discussion.

Without much delay, Rusticus and Severus were called into the throne room, crossing the threshold of a single large slab of white Grecian marble and passing through the entrance door flanked by two large columns of a deep yellow Numidian marble mottled with pink.

Two Praetorian Guard soldiers flanked the entrance, dressed in civilian togas with swords concealed underneath. Republican forms adopted by the first Emperor Augustus were still in use, particularly by an Emperor like Marcus Aurelius who was noted for being *civiliter* -- acting in a civilian manner. His practice was to treat everyone as a fellow citizen and hope, without much expectation, that he would be treated that way by them. So the protocol was no bowing and scraping in his presence, not even standing while he sat. If Aurelius sat, so should the people who were attending him. That was his "imperial" protocol. He hated pomp and fawning and catering and did his best to discourage it, hopeless as that endeavor might inevitably be.

Severus took in the large throne room hall. Its walls were covered with rich marbles and a circuit of 28 Corinthian columns. Eight large niches contained large statues of basalt, the gods Hercules and Bacchus among them.

The throne itself was in a niche at the far end of the hall. Though set on a raised dais, it was not much more than a gilded *curule* camp chair of a traditional Roman magistrate of the Republic, without back or arms. The Emperor was not on it, however. He was walking about conversing with an official over a document he was holding.

Marcus Aurelius was of medium height, somewhat shorter than Severus, and his hair and beard were short trimmed and curly, in the style of the last Emperor Antoninus Pius, who Marcus Aurelius had assisted as

The

Caesar for 23 years. Severus' beard and hair were in the same style as the Emperor's, as was Rusticus'. Aurelius looked somewhat wan and a bit frailer than he appeared in public statues and paintings. He looked like he hadn't had enough sleep. He was reputed to be somewhat sickly, perhaps even a hypochondriac, but he carried himself with dignity, with *gravitas*. He was dressed, like Rusticus, in tunic with the broad stripe of the Senatorial Order and a toga with a magistrate's border.

Aurelius finished with the official and came over to Rusticus and Severus, exchanging polite words of address and greeting kisses, first with the Urban Prefect and then with Severus. His voice was low and pleasant. He smiled at Severus and said,

"How are you Marcus, are you still as good in games as you were when we were chicks on the Caelian Hill?"

Severus laughed and relaxed. "Maybe even better, *domine*. But as I remember, you were a first class ball player. *Trigon* was your game, wasn't it?"

Aurelius smiled in return. "It still is, at least when I get the time for it. My physician Galen tells me that exercising with the small ball is good for my health. So I do it. But I hope you'll excuse me for coming directly to the point of why you're here. In this job time is of the essence. Perhaps later on we will get a chance to discuss old times when we were chicks. I would like that very much."

"As would I, *domine*."

"I asked Rusticus to bring you here because he has recommended you for an important assignment. He has informed me about your clever solution to the Cyclops case two years ago and I knew how you solved the infamous murder on the steps of the Temple of Mars the Avenger a few years before that. Rusticus thinks you'll be perfect for a mission I have in mind as my personal emissary and imperial judge. As my mentor, teacher, friend and member of my *consilium,* I trust his judgment. So I hope you will agree to take on this mission. It involves traveling to Alexandria."

Severus was taken aback by this unexpected and rather stunning suggestion. "I have always wanted to travel to Alexandria and to Egypt," he managed to reply. "The Great Library, the Museum, the Pyramids, the Sphinx."

"So now you will have the opportunity. *Carpe diem,* as we say -- seize the day." Aurelius led Severus and Rusticus to an open air portico behind the *Aula Regia.*

The Emperor continued. "Someone has tried to assassinate Marcus Annius Calvus, the Prefect of Egypt. Someone put poison into his personal drinking cup. Fortunately for the Prefect, and unfortunately for another person, that other person drank from the cup by mistake and died."

"How did that happen?"

"I understand there was a drunken orgy going on and a lot of confusion. It was in the confusion that the victim took the Prefect's cup by mistake and drank from it. But the poison was intended for the Prefect."

"Why can't the authorities in Alexandria find out who did it?"

"Maybe they can, but they haven't. And Severus, we're at war with Persia, as you know, and now we're ready to launch our counterattack and take back what they won in their invasion of the Empire and more. As everyone knows, including the Persians, Egypt is our most important province because the city of Rome gets most of its grain supply from there. Any interruption there would cause a calamity here. The attempted assassination may be the result of action by the *spasaka*, the Persian secret service. You've encountered them in the past, in the Cyclops case, as I've been informed."

"But our secret service, the *curiosi*, has agents on the spot. Aren't they able to handle the situation?"

"Frankly, Severus, my *consilium* voted that we should have our own independent investigator looking into it. There is some question about the competence and trustworthiness of the authorities in Alexandria, though I believe the Prefect himself is reliable. He's a relative, as perhaps you noted from his cognomen Annius. Annius was my original cognomen, as you'll remember from our childhood when my name was Marcus Annius Verus.

"So if you agree to be my personal emissary, I will provide you with all the necessary authority. You will not just be a judge from the judicial panel of the Urban Prefect in Rome, but I will appoint you a *iudex selectus,* a special judge empowered personally by me, just like the ones I sometimes appoint to hear cases referred to the Emperor. You may also take your own staff with you, as many as you need, and you will be provided with slaves in Alexandria, though you may take some of your own along as well. In Alexandria and Egypt you will have independence to act, subject of course to the Prefect of Egypt. You will travel by warship, a fast quadrireme, with a full complement of sailors and marines, so you will also have your own personal navy and army to follow your orders and carry out your wishes. I hope you will agree to be my emissary and judge in this matter."

"I will gladly undertake this mission, *domine*. And I will add, on a personal note that my wife Artemisia will be overjoyed to travel with me to Egypt. She has been writing a biography of Cleopatra for the last five years and for her to see those places…"

"Then that's a further inducement." Aurelius escorted Severus and Rusticus back into the *Aula Regia* and to the doorway. "Please keep me informed regularly by letter about developments. I want to know what you find out."

II

A SEA VOYAGE TO ALEXANDRIA

A t the first hour of the day, under a clear and cloud-less sky, Judge Severus stood at a dock in Ostia, the port of Rome, and admired the 120 foot long, sleek quadrireme *Argo* that would take him to Egypt. Its black hull was decorated with thin green strakes along the length of its sides and red eyes were painted on a yellow background on the prow, just behind the gleam-ing bronze-clad ram in front. The rear curved upwards and was painted green and yellow. A pennant of the Misenum Fleet stood proudly next to and above the tail. While in port, the sails and masts were not set up and the oars were shipped, though their blades projected slightly from each side. Some quadriremes had four sailors to each oar arranged in one bank, and others, like he *Argo*, had two sailors to each oar arranged in two banks, the up-per bank projecting through an outrigger and the lower bank from underneath the outrigger. The ship's 170-man crew were all professional navy personnel, the rowers trained to a high level of skill to row precisely in unison to the measured beat of a drummer signaling the pace.

Severus boarded the ship up a gangplank and went into the deck cabin at the rear, lavishly appointed with silk hangings and finely woven Egyptian mats. Glycon, his slave, began unpacking his traveler's bags, while his wife Artemisia supervised her slave Galatea in unpacking her bags.

Severus, however, had eyes only for Artemisia, whose combination of intelligence and beauty never ceased to enrapture him. Though Artemisia was a Roman citizen, she had grown up in Athens and considered herself Greek. She wore her dark hair loose and flowing and her brown eyes sparkled with life. Her mind, Severus often said, was just as keen as his own and her scholarly interests just as wide and diverse.

Meanwhile, Severus' private secretary Alexander and his staff of police aides, Vulso and Straton, and court aides – judicial assessor Flaccus and court clerk Proculus -- busied themselves finding places for their belongings and sleeping areas on deck.

"Compliments of the Trierarch," saluted a sailor entering the cabin. "*Eminentissime*," he addressed Severus using an Equestrian Class honorific, "the Trierarch Tiberius Valens requests you join him on the poop deck when you have a moment."

Judge Severus acknowledged the message and put on a cloak. He then left the cabin, inhaled the salty sea air and shivered a bit as a wind picked up. He was escorted to the captain's chair on the rear deck. The Trierarch was standing under his canopy, waiting to greet the judge. He was dressed only in a light sailor's tunic and his rugged face and physique showed the sea weather had long ago etched itself on his body, as a natural part of him.

"Tiberius Valens," saluted the ship's captain. "Trierarch of the *Argo*." The judge exchanged a polite greeting kiss with the seaman. "I'll get directly to the point," began Valens. "My orders are to get you to Alexandria as fast as possible. Then I'm to remain in the harbor with my ship and crew at your disposal."

Severus nodded affirmatively.

"In that case," continued the Trierarch, "I would appreciate knowing what our mission is. The Prefect of the Misenum Fleet said I would find out from you, *eminentissime*."

"There has been an attempt to assassinate the Prefect of Egypt," said Severus directly, "and I've been personally assigned by the Emperor to find out who did it and to make sure the Prefect stays alive."

The Trierarch looked grave.

"Your ship, Trierarch, is assigned to me for the duration of my mission. The entire crew, both sailors and marines, will remain available for shore duty and the ship will tie up in Alexandria harbor, ready at a moment's notice for rapid communication with Rome or anywhere else I might have to send you. As the Emperor himself put it to me, I'll have my own personal army and navy on this mission."

Severus reached into his cloak and pulled out a rolled up document, bearing an impressive Imperial Seal. "SPQR" it said on it. The four letters conveyed the full authority of the State, *Senatus Populusque Romanus*, the Senate and the People of Rome. Emperors deliberately spoke in the name of the Republic.

The judge handed the document to the Trierarch. Valens took his written orders and saluted the judge. "At your service, *eminentissime*"

And at his command, the ship slipped its moorings, and to the rhythm of a drummer began its fast two-week voyage from the port of Rome to *Alexandria ad Aegyptum*, Alexandria at Egypt. The oars were now projected fully outward and moved in their two banks in drilled unison to take the warship out to sea. In short order, Severus felt the up and down and forward motion of the moving vessel, heard and saw the spray shoot up around the sides and felt it vaporize in the air about him. Half the passengers were already seasick.

For the next ten days the war galley headed at maximum speed for Egypt. When the winds were favorable, the crew plied the halyards, raised the booms and billowed out the sails. One large sail amidship and a smaller one raking over the prow powered the vessel through the water at a fast 8 knots, while two large stern rudders, one on either side of the ship, guided its course. When the wind subsided, the oars sprung out in their two banks on each side and the quadrireme churned through the sea like a hundred-foot-long centipede, while the drummer, keeping time, sounded the beast's call.

The galley hugged the west coast of Italy to Messina in Sicily, sailing by day and stopping at a shore by night. Then it darted across the open sea to the north coast of Africa, making landfall at Lepcis Magna in the Province of Numidia. From there, it turned east and hugged the shore again, sailing and rowing along the coast of Cyrenaica toward Egypt.

The weather remained perfect for the length of the voyage. The sea was calm, but breezy during the day, and the nights were all wonderfully clear and fresh. For the passengers it was a welcome vacation from the stifling heat, humidity and smog of Rome, except for the time they spent being seasick.

During the days, Judge Severus, his wife and his staff enjoyed the voyage, walking the deck, basking in the sun, reading, talking together, touring the warship and just contemplating the sea. At nights they spent long hours gazing at the Moon, the planets and the stars and, prompted by Severus, talking about astronomy. It was one of his favorite subjects. He had studied it seriously ever since childhood.

Artemisia regaled the company with tales of Egypt. She read to them from Herodotus' account of his visit to Egypt 600 years earlier and the peculiar customs of Egyptians he noticed or was told about or made up. Many customs, he pointed out, were the opposite of the practices of Greeks and Romans, among others. According to Herodotus, everywhere in the world men urinated standing up while women squatted. Except in Egypt. There men squatted to pee, while women stood up. Everywhere in the world people kneaded bread dough with their hands and clay with their feet. Except in Egypt. There Egyptians kneaded the dough with their feet, but clay with their hands. In mourning, many peoples shaved their heads, while Egyptians let their hair grow. A lot of mirth accompanied her readings.

More mirth accompanied Severus' reading of Juvenal's satire on Egypt. "Who doesn't know what monstrosities demented Egypt worships? One part adores the crocodile, another quakes before the ibis that gorges itself on snakes…another worships the shining golden effigy of the long-tailed monkey. Here cats, there river fish, there whole towns venerate a dog…but it is an impious outrage to chomp to pieces leeks and onions…"

"Maybe," quipped the judge's legal assessor Flaccus, "we should turn around and go home right now."

The evening before their arrival in Alexandria, Judge Severus called a conference in his cabin. His wife and all his aides attended. Alexander, the judge's former slave and present private secretary, lit the oil lamps with a sulfur match. He was a slim man and though middle aged, he looked boyish. His professional training and experience as a librarian and his deep interest in books and knowledge could almost be seen in the fine features of his face and the faraway look in his eyes. Alexander was more excited by an interesting fact than most people were by a victory of their favorite gladiator in the arena.

The two military members of the judge's staff came in first. Caius Vulso, a Centurion, and Publius Aelianus Straton, a lower ranked Tesserarius, were both members of Rome's Urban Cohort and carried out the police work in the judge's criminal investigations. They were, however, quite different.

Vulso, an army veteran, had served 20 years with the legions in Europe, Asia and Africa. He was resourceful, tough and smart in the ways of the world. And since his military career had included a stint with the Legion II Traiana Fortis, stationed in Nikopolis, four miles east of Alexandria, he would be particularly useful on this mission.

Vulso was big and strong with broad shoulders and legs like columns. He sported a short, clipped military beard and his features were somewhat brutal, as he himself sometimes was, but he had educated himself and was naturally clever. He carried out his tasks for the judge one way or another. No one would want to tangle with him.

Straton was average height and wiry. He had not come to the Urban Cohort after retirement from the army. Rather as a child he had been a slave in the imperial household of the Emperor Hadrian and had been freed upon Hadrian's death. He automatically became a Roman citizen upon manumission by a Roman citizen but he never lost his animosity towards those people whose slave he had been. Still, Straton was expert at undercover assignments, his average looks and sad brown eyes allowing him to blend in almost anywhere. He could pose as anyone from a wandering philosopher to a carriage driver to a slave to a member of the imperial household.

He and Vulso admired each other's skills and competence, and were friends, but they disliked each other's attitudes. Vulso deliberately projected himself as a proud and aggressive Roman; Straton saw himself as a subtle and cynical Greek.

Both men exchanged greeting kisses with the judge and Alexander and plunked down in chairs. Vulso grabbed an apple from a fruit bowl on a table. It had just been taken out of its crate and still felt cool from the snow it had been packed in.

"Where's Flaccus and Proculus?" asked the Centurion, taking a huge bite.

"They'll be here any moment," replied Severus.

Artemisia was intently studying a map of Alexandria, unfurled on her lap. "Where is the Hadrianum, Vulso?" she asked. "The place where we're staying."

"Near the center," replied Vulso. "Between Caesar's Palace and the Claudium."

"Now I see it," said Artemisia, moving her finger to a spot on the map. "And the Hadrianum houses the Roman government?"

"Yes. Most of the offices and apartments of officials are there. We'll probably be assigned rooms there ourselves."

"I expect it's a beautiful building," commented Artemisia, "if the Emperor Hadrian had it built. He probably designed it himself."

"It is a beautiful building," replied Vulso. "It's adorned with galleries, libraries, porches, courts, halls, walks, groves, as well as choice paintings, mosaics and statues. I'm sure you'll like it."

"And where was Cleopatra's palace? I have to spend some time there in researching my biography of her."

"I'm not sure, but I think it was in the same area."

The curtain parted and Gaius Sempronius Flaccus, the judge's judicial assessor, and Quintus Proculus, his court clerk, entered the cabin. Flaccus was a young man, now five years out of the law school of Sabinus and Cassius, the same school Severus had attended, as did his father and his father before him. Flaccus had served as Severus' assessor right out of law school and was endowed with a quick wit, irreverent humor and a good legal mind.

Quintus Proculus was in his late sixties. He took down judicial proceedings in 'Tironian Notes' shorthand, supervised the court records, prepared legal documents, and oversaw the court slaves. He was a stickler for detail and had a deep respect for the protocols of a Roman court. Having spent his life in the courts, he knew more about law than most lawyers – and most judges as well.

When polite greetings had been exchanged and everyone was comfortably seated, Judge Severus opened the meeting.

"Since we arrive in Alexandria tomorrow morning," he began, "I thought it would be a good thing if we had a briefing. The trip has been a little vacation so far, but we should now consider the investigation officially underway."

There were nods of agreement all around.

"So far I've only told you the purpose of our mission -- to capture the person who tried to kill the Prefect of Egypt and prevent any other attempts on the Prefect's life. Now, I'd like to tell you the details of the case as I know them."

The flickering oil lamps, the creaking ship and the slurping of the water filled a pause. The judge took a sip of spicy red wine.

"It's slightly embarrassing for the Prefect," said Severus with a wry grin. "The attempt on his life was made at an orgy. Someone put poison in his wine cup. However, in the confusion of the orgy, his wine was drunk by a man on the next couch, an official of the Imperial Post – the *Cursus Publicus* - named Titus Pudens. Pudens dropped dead on the spot."

Severus took a sheet of papyrus from a file on his lap and unfurled it. "I have a list of the guests."

He scanned it quickly to refresh his memory and then let it roll up. "The orgy was held in the Prefect's private apartment in the Hadrianum. Including the Prefect, there were seven men and seven women. All the women were professional *hetairai*, from the finest and most exclusive house in Alexandria."

"Which one?" asked Vulso.

"The House of Selene," answered the judge. "Do you know it?"

"I know of it," replied the Centurion. "When I was with the Legion II Traiana Fortis some of the wealthy officers would often mention it with appreciation. But it's too rich for my tastes and the women are too intellectual."

"Vulso prefers the ones around the docks," quipped Flaccus.

Vulso guffawed, along with everyone else.

"The dead man, Pudens," continued Severus, "was one of the guests. He was an inspector in the Imperial Post in Alexandria. It seems he was the guest of honor at the orgy.

"Also present was the Prefect's stepson and personal aide, a young man named Secundus.

"Then there was a man named Philogenes. He's a Homeric scholar on the staff of the Great Library of Alexandria."

"I'm glad to see," commented Vulso, "that he has other interests besides books."

Alexander, the former librarian, gave Vulso a fishy look.

"Then," continued the judge, there was an Egyptian, a Priest of Isis, named Petamon.

"I thought priests of Isis are supposed to be celibate," sneered Straton.

"Apparently," remarked Flaccus, "this one hasn't heard about it."

"Of the final two guests at the orgy, one Isarion is an antique dealer in Alexandria. It seems the Prefect is a collector. The other, Serpentinus, is a member of the Prefect's staff."

"Serpentinus? A snake?" commented Flaccus. "I suspect him already."

Severus put the file on a low table next to his chair.

"The Prefect, as you all know, is a very important person. Not only does he hold the second highest government post reserved for Equestrians, after the Prefect of Praetorians, but he governs the most important province in the Empire. Because of its huge grain supply that feeds the dole for the city of Rome, Egypt is not an ordinary province. It is a personal possession of the Emperor and no one of the Senatorial Class is allowed in without written permission – a visa – from the Emperor."

"No senators subverting the stability of the imperial regime," commented Vulso with sarcasm in his voice.

"The Prefecture of Egypt," continued Severus, "is the culmination of a lifetime career of outstanding government service and no one attains that post without good reason. Marcus Annius Calvus, the present Prefect, and the intended victim of the assassination, held a series of high government jobs, both in Rome and the provinces, before his present post. He has a reputation as an administrative and tax expert. Though held in esteem in government circles, he may of course have made personal enemies through his official actions and we'll have to be

26 Marcus Aurelius Betrayed

probing along these lines in our investigation. We'll also have to keep in mind the possibility that this was a political assassination attempt, either done by or at the behest of the Persians or maybe even for internal Egyptian reasons. Remember, we're at war with Persia, and the *spasaka*, the 'Eye of the Great King' may be active in Egypt. And there also has been frequent internal strife in Alexandria.

"Alexandria has a deserved reputation for being a hotbed of civil disorder. As Vulso can undoubtedly tell you, the city has three large population groups, Greeks, Jews and Egyptians, and they have a long history of rioting against each other, in every conceivable combination. And the Roman administration always gets caught in the middle."

"When I was there," commented Vulso, "about ten years ago, the Prefect was killed during one of those outbreaks. An entire legion had to be called in to restore order."

There was a commotion on deck and shouts could be heard. Vulso shot up and went out. He came back a few moments later. "We've sighted the lighthouse," he announced.

Everyone, sailors and passengers alike, rushed toward the prow. 25 miles away, on the dark horizon, was what looked like a bright star. The fire from the great Pharos lighthouse, kindled almost 500 feet above ground and beamed far out to sea by a huge reflecting mirror, blazed brightly, a beacon in the night.

III

THE PREFECT OF EGYPT

The guards slammed their hobnailed boots onto the marble floor and stood to attention. The chamberlain opened an imposing bronze studded wood door and announced, "The Most Eminent Marcus Flavius Severus, imperial emissary and special judge of the Emperor."

Severus strode into the Prefect's office. It was a large airy room, beautifully decorated with marbled floor and walls and furnished with plush couches, rare wood tables and cases for books and documents. The Prefect put down a scroll and came over to greet his visitor. The two men exchanged greeting kisses, while slaves helped Severus out of his formal toga.

"It's a pleasure to meet you," said the Prefect. "I trust your accommodations are satisfactory and that you slept well."

Severus replied that they were and he had, although in fact he had hardly slept at all. He and Artemisia had been so excited to actually be in Egypt that they stayed up half the night talking and making love.

But Severus merely the exchanged light pleasantries with Calvus about the sea voyage.

Marcus Annius Calvus was a vigorous man, about 60-years-old, with a short beard and graying hair. He visibly projected the power and authority he wielded. His whole manner exuded confidence and consciousness of his position and rank.

Calvus motioned the judge to one of the two white-cushioned reclining couches, while taking the other for himself. Slaves unobtrusively placed wine and fruit on a low table between the couches and left the room. Severus took in more of the office. Two portrait paintings of the co-Emperors Marcus Aurelius and Lucius Verus hung prominently behind the Prefect's desk and a variety of small objects of art were tastefully displayed on tables and in wall niches. Folding doors opened onto a balcony and Severus caught a glimpse of a lush garden outside and beyond it the sea. He settled onto the couch in a reclining position.

"And how is the Emperor?" asked the Prefect chattily, as he settled onto his couch.

Severus hardly knew how to answer the question. Aside from their childhood acquaintance, his meeting with Marcus Aurelius had been business-like and lasted less than half an hour. But Calvus was a relative of Marcus Aurelius and his manner indicated that he was a personal friend of the Emperor and expected the imperial emissary was also.

"He's worried about the war," replied Severus, recounting the talk in the City.

"I would be too," replied the Prefect, "although after our initial defeats, we should be ready to take the offensive by now. The European legions have arrived in the East, Avidius Cassius has whipped the eastern army into shape, and we're ready to counterattack. But it's shaping up as the biggest war in fifty years. For a new Emperor, I'm not surprised he's worried."

The Prefect's bodyguard, a huge man, came in and placed a group of documents on the table in front of him. "These are the emissary's credentials," he informed Calvus, "and the dispatches he brought with him."

The Prefect glanced at them. There was a *diploma* granting Severus full judicial authority within the jurisdiction of Egypt, subject to that of the Prefect himself. It included powers to investigate, arrest, conduct judicial trials and impose punishments, including the power to impose the death penalty. Another document specifically defined Severus' mission in Egypt as the discovery of the Prefect's would-be assassin and, as a corollary, the protection of the Prefect from further attempts on his life. Calvus read that one carefully, holding it close to his eyes and squinting at some passages.

He finished, put it down, and stared at Judge Severus for a long moment. "We were informed by Imperial Post that you were being sent out, but I'm afraid that you've come in vain."

Severus looked at him inquiringly.

"You see, Judge Severus, we already have him. The person who tried to poison me has already been arrested, tried and executed!"

IV

GANYMEDE'S CONFESSION

Judge Severus sat upright on his couch. "You've already caught him? When? Who was it?"

Calvus waved his hand airily. "It was one of my slaves. He confessed under judicial torture. He had a personal grudge against me. Seems that the deluded wretch was having fantasies that I was sleeping with his wife." The Prefect shrugged his shoulders. "She had once been my concubine, it's true. But when I tired of her, I gave her to Ganymede. He was consumed by an insane jealousy. The gods must have possessed him."

The Prefect took a sip of wine. "We executed him over a week ago."

Severus was stunned.

"I'll show you the confession," Calvus continued. "You'll have to make a complete report to Rome, naturally. Other than that, I suppose you could reasonably spend a few weeks in Egypt as a tourist before heading back." The Prefect shrugged again. "I'm sorry you had to travel so far for nothing. But I wrote to Rome about it. I suppose my message reached the Palatine while you were on route."

Calvus rose from his couch, took a last sip of wine, handed Severus back his credentials and escorted him to the door. "Naturally, Severus, you and your wife will be my guests at dinner tonight. I want to hear more about your pleasant sea voyage."

The Prefect rapped on the door. It was opened by a young man clad in a toga, stylishly and fancily made up with gold dust in his hair. He was shorter than Severus in height and on the thin side and had a clever look about him. Several clerks entered the room and began setting up for a meeting.

"I'll leave you in the hands of Secundus here," said Calvus. "Secundus is not only my personal aide but he is also my stepson, soon to be adopted as my son. I appointed him *iudex selectus*, special judge, and he personally conducted the investigation and trial of the case you're interested in."

The Prefect addressed the young man. "Secundus, this is Marcus Flavius Severus, the imperial emissary and special judge from Rome, appointed personally by the Emperor to find out who tried to kill me. Of course, he didn't know we've already concluded the case, but he will naturally want to see Ganymede's confession. And any other arrangements he'll need, you can take care of."

He turned back to Severus. "Secundus will arrange the tours for you to the famous sights of Alexandria. I expect you'll also want to spend some time up-country in Egypt, seeing the Pyramids, the Sphinx, the tombs of the pharaohs and all the other ancient wonders."

Severus thanked him and the Prefect went back into his office.

"A terrible thing," said Secundus to the judge as he escorted him down the marbled hall to his office. "'So many slaves, so many enemies', as they say. The Prefect was lucky. It was only by a fluke that Ganymede didn't succeed."

The corridors were bustling with toga-clad officials and slaves and clerks in tunics, all carrying papers to and fro, animatedly discussing things or just looking important.

"How did you single out Ganymede?" asked Severus. "Was his hostility toward the Prefect a matter of common knowledge in the household?"

"No," answered Secundus. "We simply started to torture all the slaves who serviced the party and also had an opportunity to handle the wine or get near the Prefect's cup. Ganymede confessed."

Severus glared at him. Torturing someone without having some specific suspicion of his guilt was illegal according to a rescript of the Emperor Hadrian.

Secundus brought the judge into his office, rummaged through a pile of files on a table, pulled one out, and extracted a sheet of papyrus. Here's the confession."

"I, Ganymede, slave of Prefect Marcus Annius Calvus, do hereby confess that on the night of the Ides of May, I put poison in the drinking cup of my master, the cup with the dolphins. I confess I intended to kill my master.

"Because I thought my wife Theodora was unfaithful to me with the Prefect, I wanted to kill the Prefect. I now know I was wrong in this belief.

"I procured the poison from an Egyptian sorceress named Phna. Her shop is in the Rhakotis Section of the City, near the Moon Gate. I procured it five days before the Ides of May and waited for an opportunity to use it. I put it in my master's drinking cup a few minutes after the entertainment began. I did not put it in anyone else's cup.

"I am sorry that the wrong person died and I wish to be executed for what I did."

> "/s/ Ganymede, slave of
> Marcus Annius Calvus."

Severus looked up. "Have the local police, the *phylakes*, spoken to this sorceress, Phna? Did she corroborate the confession?"

"She denied it, of course," answered Secundus. "I questioned her myself. Oh, she admits Ganymede was a customer of hers. But she denies it was poison he bought. She claims she never deals in poison. Only herbs and magic potions. She said she often mixed love potions for Ganymede. But everyone knows all these old women deal in poisons too. Only she'll never admit it to the authorities. The law against poisoners, you know."

Severus glanced through the rest of the file. There was a list of the other slave who had been tortured, a report of an interview with the sorceress Phna confirming what Secundus had said, a list of the guests at the orgy with a diagram of the seating arrangements, and the court documents -- the charge sheet, the trial extracts, the judgment and the order of execution. Ganymede had been beheaded. There was also a painting of a thin, old man, with a weak chin and a balding head.

"Is this Ganymede?" asked Severus.

"Yes," answered Secundus. "A police artist did it to show around to witnesses during the investigation."

"Who else was questioned?"

"Everyone at the party, naturally. The guests and the women."

Severus leafed through the file a second time. "I don't see any affidavits from any of them and from a quick glance at the trial extract, none of them were witnesses."

"It wasn't necessary," said Secundus casually. "No one had any information and the confession was all we needed."

Severus closed the file. He looked straight at Secundus. "I'm sure you know that the law requires corroboration of evidence extracted by torture."

"I know that. But there is corroboration. The sorceress Phna sold Ganymede potions."

"But she didn't admit selling him poison. She denied it. So how can that be corroboration?" asked Severus, his face twisting up in an unpleasant expression. Secundus simply shrugged with an unconcerned look on his face.

"I was the judge at his trial," declared Secundus, "and the evidence showed he was guilty. He confessed and I followed all the correct procedures even to turning my toga inside out when delivering the death sentence."

Severus got up to leave. "I'll take this file with me, if you don't mind."

Secundus nodded in assent.

"By the way," added Severus, "I would like to have a word with Ganymede's wife. She's still the property of the Prefect, isn't she? I'm sure the Prefect wouldn't mind me talking to her under the circumstances."

"No, I'm sure he wouldn't. But she's no longer in Alexandria. She was sent to the Prefect's estate in Sicily after Ganymede was executed." Secundus walked the judge to the door. "The poor fool was deluded. We all felt sorry for him." He pointed to the file in the judge's hand. "You might have seen in the order of execution that we allowed Ganymede to be beheaded. It was really quite a consideration on the part of the Prefect to proscribe the most lenient form of the death penalty, usually reserved for members of the Senatorial and Equestrian Classes -- for *honestiores*. Slaves don't usually get off so lightly."

Severus was escorted by a slave to the suite of apartments assigned to him and his staff. Everyone was waiting in the atrium and he rapidly briefed them on what he had learned that morning.

"A few free weeks in Egypt," said Flaccus, smiling broadly. "Where will we go tomorrow?"

"I think we'll tour Alexandria," replied Severus, "except for Vulso and Straton."

"And what are we going to do?" asked the Centurion.

"It looks like we've been called back from the finish line to the starting gate, as the saying goes." He held up Ganymede's confession. "This has to be corroborated before I and Roman law are satisfied. And so far there is not one iota of corroboration. The starting gate is the orgy itself and the people who attended. So tomorrow I want you to find the House of Selene and set up a conference for the day after tomorrow with all the *hetairai* who attended the orgy."

V

THE *SOMA* AND THE GREAT
LIBRARY OF ALEXANDRIA

While Vulso and Straton were off to the House of Selene, the judge, Artemisia, his assessor Flaccus, Alexander and Proculus spent the morning as tourists, walking about the city and seeing some of Alexandria's famous sights.

Unlike most cities, with their narrow streets and jumbled arrangement of houses and buildings evolved over time in a more or less random way, Alexandria was a city planned from its inception on a grid pattern. Alexander the Great and his architect Dinocrates had walked the uninhabited site spreading grain on the ground to mark off the walls and streets. The central streets, the Canopic Way and the Street of the Soma, were wide and colonnaded. The Canopic Way ran parallel to the Mediterranean and was 90 feet wide, broad enough for eight chariots to drive side by side. Streets running perpendicular to the sea were arranged in just such a way as to catch the northern breeze blowing in from the Mediterranean.

Severus and his group started their sight-seeing at
the central intersection of the two main streets where the
Soma -- the 'body'of Alexander the Great -- was preserved and entombed. The embalmed body of the Greek
world's most renowned hero and founder of the city
lay enclosed in a crystal coffin, where every day lines
of tourists filed by. The central square had been made
even more impressive by the Roman Emperor Vespasian
with the addition of a Tetrapylon, a square pavilion in-
corporating four arches, each one spanning one of the
entrances to the square.

The body of Alexander had been brought to Egypt
by Ptolemy I, one of his Royal Companions from youth
in Macedon, who had later become one of Alexander's
trusted generals during the conquest of the Persian
Empire. After Alexander's untimely death at the age of
33, several of his generals divided up the conquests between them. Ptolemy chose Egypt and while the body
of Alexander had been slated to go back to Macedon for
burial, Ptolemy had hijacked it on route, brought it to
Alexandria and entombed it in a golden coffin as a cen-
terpiece to the city. A later Ptolemy, short of money, sold
the gold coffin and replaced it with the crystal coffin, still
honorable, but less costly. When the great Caius Julius
Caesar came to Alexandria and began his liaison with
Cleopatra, he came to the *Soma* to pay respects and was
moved to tears. Now 200 years later, Severus and his
entourage merely ambled by, looking but not weeping.

After the *Soma*, the group ascended the Paneion. A
sanctuary to the god Pan, it was an unusual structure,
shaped like a fir-cone and resembling a rocky hill, with
a spiral road leading to the top. In the clear, cloudless

day, they had a magnificent view of the city, spread out below.

To the north was the lustrous blue-green Mediterranean Sea shimmering in the sun, with the Lighthouse on Pharos Island jutting high into the air. The Lighthouse was the second tallest structure in the world, only a few feet shorter than the Great Pyramid outside Memphis. Each was one of the Seven Wonders of the World according to the list compiled by Antipater of Sidon. The Lighthouse was one Ptolemy I's great ideas, along with Alexandria's Great Library and the Museum.

The Lighthouse was built of white marble, limestone and pink Aswan granite. Almost 500 feet tall, its first stage rose about 300 feet from a solid square pedestal, 100 feet on all four sides. From there a second stage, octagonal in shape, rose another 100 feet and had an observation deck for tourists. The third stage was circular in shape and rose another 100 feet into the sky. This was topped by the round fire chamber where a burning flame was converted into the Lighthouse beacon by a huge bronze reflecting mirror.

The tallest building in Rome was the 10-story *insula* apartment house of Felicula in Regio IX, the Campus Martius Region of the City. But the Pharos Lighthouse was 5 times as tall.

"When are we going to climb it?" said Artemisia to her husband as they marveled at its height.

"We'll set aside a day to climb it," replied Severus. "After all, we promised the children to tell them what it was like from the top."

Looking away from the Lighthouse and the harbor, the sprawl of the city below was a vision in white marble and red roof tiles. They could pick out palaces, theaters, gymnasia, temples, stadiums and lush green garden areas.

To the west were the Egyptian quarter, Rhakotis, and the Moon Gate, while to the east were the Jewish sections, the Delta and Beta quarters, near the Sun Gate. In the center was the Brucheion, the Greek and Roman section of the city. The two obelisks the Emperor Augustus brought from Egyptian Thebes to grace the Caesareum in the Roman area rose prominently and majestically into the sky.

In the South, beyond Serapeum Hill, with its monumental rectangular temple to Isis and Serapis, were the clear blue waters of Lake Mareotis, and beyond that the fabled lands of Egypt.

Their views and walk through the city made clear the unique feel of Alexandria. It was not just that the city was crowded with life and teeming with activity. So was Rome, so was Antioch and Athens and other great cities of the Empire. Nor was it the congestion, though Alexandria wasn't as bad as Rome even though, unlike Rome, Alexandria allowed chariots and wagons and horses on the streets during the day. Nor was it the virtual absence of togas, since the majority of the populace wore Greek style tunics – *peplos, chiton* – and a *himation* over the tunics. Severus and Artemisia were used to that since Artemisia grew up in Athens and Severus lived there in his student days.

Rather it was first the large in-mixture of Egyptian things: Egyptian obelisks and temples and paintings and art and Egyptian people wearing Egyptian style clothing. There were also many people from African lands like Nubia and Ethiopia, and a large number of people from other eastern lands dressed in their ethnic clothing – Babylonians, Syrians, Jews, Indians, even people from distant parts of Asia like Bactria and even beyond. Rome had all of these too, of course, but not in nearly the numbers; in Rome they were often just oddities, in Alexandria an integral part of the city.

Everyone, for instance, was fascinated by the sight of priests from India in saffron robes; they had been trying to spread the teachings of the Buddha in Alexandria since Ptolemaic times.

Also there were the special animals on the street in Alexandria. Not just the large number of cats, which were beloved and hugely respected in Egypt, but also cobra snakes and snake charmers. And then there were the ibises, the beautiful long-legged large yellow beaked white birds who could often be seen down side streets searching for and finding garbage to eat. Rome had cats, but rarely a snake charmer and no ibises.

Judge Severus and his party contemplated and commented on the views for a long time and then returned to the Hadrianum for lunch and an after-lunch siesta.

At the 9th hour of the day, they all headed to the nearby Library of Alexandria, the greatest library in the world, where the Prefect had arranged a special tour for the imperial emissary. "A Sanitarium for the Mind" said the inscription above the entrance to the Great Library. Judge Severus and his entourage gawked up at the famous phrase for a few moments. Then Proculus went inside to give the judge's name to the library staff, and the judge was then met at the door by a distinguished looking elderly man with a short white beard. He was impeccably dressed in a Greek style *chiton*, white with a red meander pattern on the hem. He introduced himself in Latin as Creon, one of the library staff and their tour guide "for the Most Eminent guest of the Prefect."

Severus, speaking Greek, introduced Artemisia, Flaccus and Alexander, as Creon led them into the library's main hall. It was magnificent -- a vast room with a high ceiling decorated with intricately carved and gilded rare woods. A beautiful white marble floor with colorful mosaics displayed the high bookcases lining the hall. Each bookcase was divided horizontally and vertically into pigeon-hole shelves, in which volumes of scrolls were arranged. Labels dangling from the scrolls announced the title of the book in bright red letters. Ladders on rollers were interspersed against the bookcases, allowing access to the higher shelves, while elegant tables and chairs were occupied by scholars, researchers and interested people who used the library.

"The Library of Alexandria," said Creon, continuing in Greek, "is the greatest library in the world, containing more than 500,000 volumes in two buildings. This one, the 'Mother Library', contains most of the collection, while an additional 50,000 volumes are located in the 'Daughter Library' in the Serapeum Temple on Serapeum Hill, south of the city walls."

They strolled about the hall, looking this way and that, while Creon continued his patter.

"The Library was founded 470 years ago by Ptolemy I Soter, Alexander the Great's Royal Companion and general, who wanted to make Alexandria the rival of Athens. With the help and advice of the Athenian, Demetrius of

Phaleron, a student of Aristotle, Ptolemy invited the greatest philosophers and most learned men in Greece to settle
in Alexandria and live and study and work at the Museum,
an institute for research and learning. The Library was actually conceived as an adjunct to the Museum and was
founded with the intention of gathering all the books in the
world, both Greek and non-Greek.

"Ptolemy, as you may recall, was not only one of
Alexander's generals, but as boys in Macedon had also been
one of Alexander's designated Royal Companions. As you
know, Alexander was tutored by Aristotle, so Ptolemy, as
one of the Companions, was a student of Aristotle along
with him. It's my personal opinion that since Ptolemy was
two years older than Alexander, he got more out of being
taught by Aristotle even than did Alexander. In any event,
Ptolemy always said that it was Aristotle who was the real
inspiration for the Museum and Library."

The tour guide led them to a shelf and plucked a scroll
from its compartment. "This hall contains the famous
120 volume catalogue of all the books in the Library.
The first catalogue, a masterpiece of scholarly achieve-
ment, was compiled by Callimachus, the renowned poet
and first librarian."

He opened the scroll and showed them how to use
the catalogue. "The books in the catalogue are divided into eight classes: Epic and Lyric Poetry; Laws;
Philosophy; History; Oratory; Rhetoric; and finally a
Miscellaneous class which is further subdivided into
Medicine, Mathematical studies, Philosophy of Nature
and non-Greek books."

"How extensive is the non-Greek collection?" asked
Alexander.

"A good question," replied Creon. "The Library has always had a continuing program to translate the principal works of other peoples into Greek. It now contains the major works of the Romans, the Egyptians, the Jews, the Babylonians and the Indians, as well as a variety of works from other languages, such as Punic and Aramaic."

Creon led the group into a second hall. It was not as large as the first, but it was no less elegantly furnished. "The Ten Halls are divided by subject matter. This is the 'Hall of the Philosophy of Nature,' the special creation of the great astronomer-librarians Eratosthenes and Aristarchus."

"Can books be taken out?" asked Flaccus. "In Rome some libraries allow it and some don't."

"Scholars in residence at the Museum can do so, of course, and we have a circulating collection for others with a library pass."

The tour continued through the remainder of the Halls, with Creon noting items of interest, giving background sketches of some of the books and writers whose works were preserved there. He explained that the Library's huge collection was built up over the years by the expedient of examining every ship that came to Alexandria for books, taking whatever they found, making copies and then returning the original or a copy to the owner.

"How bad was the fire," asked Artemisia. "The one which destroyed part of the library during the uprising against Cleopatra, when Caesar set fire to the ships in the harbor."

"This building wasn't touched, fortunately," replied Creon. "Burning masts fell into the streets around the docks and burned up a very large collection of books waiting shipment from our Library to Rome. It was a disaster, of course, but as you can see, our collection is still intact."

Artemisia added a fact from her study of Cleopatra. "Didn't Marcus Antonius later take 200,000 volumes from the library at Pergamum and give them as a present to Cleopatra to make up for the books lost in that fire?"

"Indeed, yes," answered Creon with slightly distasteful expression.

Judge Severus thanked Creon "for the pleasant and informative tour" and then asked if he would introduce him to Philogenes. The judge had no prejudice against mixing business with pleasure and Philogenes had been one of the guests at the Prefect's orgy. "I understand that Philogenes is a Homeric scholar on the library staff."

"I know him, of course," replied Creon. "He's not only an eminent and learned Homeric scholar but an assistant to the Keeper of the Books. However I'm afraid you won't be able to meet him. He's not here again today."

"Oh," said Severus. "Perhaps another time."

"I hope so," answered Creon. "No one has seen him for the past week. He hasn't been to work or, from what I hear, at his home either."

The judge arched his eyebrows.

"He seems to have disappeared," said Creon.

VI

AT THE APARTMENT OF PHILOGENES

While Artemisia, Alexander and Proculus headed back to the Hadrianum to rest and get ready for dinner, Judge Severus and Flaccus hired a litter outside the Library and told the bearers to take them to an address near the Temple of Bendis. According to the library staff, it was where Philogenes lived.

Philogenes lived on the second floor of a modest four-story apartment house. The slave doorman sitting at the entrance told them that Philogenes hadn't been there for a week, but that his two slaves were upstairs. Severus and Flaccus quickly climbed the stairs, knocked on the door and were greeted by an old woman.

"The Prefect has sent me to find Philogenes," announced Severus in Greek in a commanding tone. "I want to talk to you and whoever is living here."

The old woman melted out of the way and the two men entered. A young girl stood inside. She was strikingly beautiful, with dark hair and dark eyes and looked no more than 15 or 16-years-old.

The room itself was modestly furnished with a table and chairs. A curtain shielded the entrance to another room and the walls were painted with scenes from Homer. A small table in the corner contained an object that caught the judge's eye. It was a small and very old-looking statue of an Egyptian Pharaoh or nobleman, sculpted in common black basalt. Severus inspected it more closely. Although the figure was in an ordinary, stylized Egyptian pose -- one foot in front of the other, arms at the side, head framed by a headdress falling to the neck -- it was nonetheless a remarkable piece. The artist had somehow breathed life into it, and to Severus the figure seemed to be in the act of walking right off its pedestal. He thought it must have been very old and very expensive.

"Where did your master get this?" asked Severus casually, as if trying to put the two slaves at their ease.

"From the antique dealer Isarion," answered the old woman. "It was a gift. The master prizes it highly."

"I can see why," commented Severus, still studying the statue, while mentally noting the name of the antique dealer Isarion, another of the guests at the Prefect's orgy.

The young slave girl brought fruit and wine to a table and the old woman motioned for the two men to sit and refresh themselves.

"Does your master have any other antiques," asked Severus.

"Oh yes," said the young girl. "He has a whole chest full of antiquities. But it's locked."

The judge left the statue regretfully and took a seat at the table where Flaccus and the two women were waiting for him.

"Where is your master?" asked Severus gently.

"We don't know," answered the old woman. She took a handkerchief from the palm of her hand and wiped her eyes. "He left seven days ago and hasn't returned."

"Where did he say he was going?"

"He left after dinner. He didn't say where he was going. He only said that he had to meet someone and would be back late."

"Does he have family or friends he could be staying with?"

"We checked. No one knows where he is," answered the old woman. "He hasn't been to work and the police – the *phylakes* -- can't find him. We're very worried."

"Has anything like this happened before?"

They both held up their hands and jerked back their heads in negative gestures.

"Was he worried about anything?" asked the judge. "Was anything disturbing him? How did he seem before he left?"

"Worried? Yes, you're right about that," said the old woman.

"Oh yes," said the young girl. "He was worried. He was worried for the past few weeks before he disappeared. He was moody around the house, not his usual self. Late at night, after I was asleep, I would sometimes wake up and find him pacing the room, back and forth. I often asked him what was wrong. But he never would tell me."

Severus thought for a moment. "Did he ever hint at what was worrying him? Money? His job? Something to do with the Prefect's party? Did he mention that to you?"

"Yes," said the old woman. "I told him he shouldn't be toadying up to all those high-class people in government.

They were out of his class. He came home from that party looking horrible. Like he had seen a ghost. He said someone tried to poison the Prefect."

"And that wasn't the only thing that worried him," interjected the young girl.

"It wasn't?"

"No. Even before the death at the party, he was really disturbed. But it was about the stolen books."

"What stolen books?" asked Severus.

"The books he was supposed to find. The ones stolen from the Library."

"Tell me about them."

"He never told me anything about it," continued the young girl. "I overheard something. I know I shouldn't be telling this, but I have to."

"You're quite right to do so," encouraged Severus.

"One night, when the man who lives next door was here for a game of 'Sacred Way' -- the master and him used to play once a week -- I was asked to come in and play the lyre during the game."

"You should hear her play," interjected the old woman. "She could be in an orchestra or perform on the stage anytime."

The young girl blushed and the judge prompted her to continue.

"Well, I heard them discussing the books. My master said that rare books had been stolen from the Library and that he was told by the Keeper of the Books to find out what happened. I think that's what was worrying him but it became worse after the Prefect's party."

Severus and Flaccus left, wondering what was going on.

VII

THE KEEPER OF THE BOOKS

There was no carefree tourism on Judge Severus' schedule the next day. The appointment at the House of Selene to interview the *hetairai* who had been at the orgy was set up for the afternoon – the women generally slept late. So in the morning, Severus and Flaccus sent a messenger to arrange an interview for him with the Keeper of the Books at the Library to discuss Philogenes. When a return message was received from the Library that the Chief Librarian would see the imperial emissary immediately, Severus and Flaccus took a litter in front of the Hadrianum and proceeded to the meeting.

Arriving at the Library, Severus and Flaccus were immediately taken to see The Keeper of the Books. He did not look like a bookish person. His overly enthusiastic welcome and ever-present smile reminded Severus of a politician or courtier, rather than of a distinguished scholar. Perhaps the job required skills in both areas.

The Keeper confirmed that there had been a disappearance of rare books from the library and that Philogenes had been assigned by him to find them. He explained that they hadn't called in the authorities because it was possible, though unlikely, that the books were misplaced, rather than stolen. But now that Philogenes had also disappeared, the Keeper was on the verge of notifying the *phylakes*.

"Your arrival," he told Severus, "is therefore most timely."

The Keeper explained that over the past few months the staff had discovered rare books gone. The discoveries had all been completely by chance. All the books were seldomly used and were, in fact, rare editions. It was only when someone happened to ask for them that their disappearance was noted, and the increasing number of missing rare editions made it look like a pattern of thievery. Moreover, the library staff responsible for the care of the missing volumes could hardly make consistent mis-filings of such valuable books.

The Keeper then provided Judge Severus with a list of the missing rare books. There was a book of poetry by the first librarian, Callimachus, said to have been his personal copy. There was also book one of an early edition of Homer's *Iliad*, and an old philosophical work by someone Severus had never heard of, Lycon of Tarentum.

"Only bibliophiles and Pythagorean scholars have heard of him," explained the librarian, "but the missing roll might be the only one in existence. That makes it very valuable."

Finally, and curiously, there was an old Jewish philosophical work, written in Hebrew, called *The Wisdom of Ben Sira*.

"I dread the fact that there may be others missing," said the librarian, "but I fear the worst."

"Did Philogenes ask you for the job of finding the missing books?" asked Severus.

The librarian caught the inference. "As a matter of fact he did. Why? Do you think he had anything to do with it?"

"I don't know. It's possible, of course, and his disappearance on top of it is suspicious. Let me think a moment."

The judge twirled his beard and lapsed into thought, while the librarian turned to some paperwork on his desk.

"I have a suggestion," said Severus finally.

The librarian looked up.

"I have a freedman with me in Alexandria. He was once a librarian himself. Beyond that, his association with me has given him an acquaintance with criminal investigations. He would be perfect to take on the job of tracking down the missing books."

"I don't know," said the Keeper uncertainly. "He's not part of the staff..."

"That's an advantage in this case," countered Severus. "He's entirely independent, as Philogenes apparently was not. Furthermore, as a personal emissary of the Emperor, I strongly suggest that you hire him for this job as a special assistant."

The Keeper of the Books noted the commanding tone and assented gracefully. "It doesn't sound like a bad idea at all, Judge Severus. Send your man to me. He can start tomorrow."

"I will," replied Severus. "His name is Alexander."

VIII

THE HOUSE OF SELENE

The House of Selene was no ordinary brothel, state run and taxed, with a fixed entrance fee, and open to the public at large. Rather it was an exclusive establishment of *hetairai* -- courtesans -- in the tradition of Old Greece, where beautiful young girls were trained in music and dance and culture as much as in the development of their physical talents. They were educated particularly to witty conversation and literary learning and were accomplished musicians on lyre or flute or cithara. They were fashioned to be apt companions for men of the first rank in the arts, government or commerce, and could grace a cultured dinner party equally as well as a bed.

Most *hetairai* looked down on ordinary women. Common prostitutes were beneath their contempt. Their models were famous courtesans of the past, such as Aspasia and Phryne. Aspasia, the mistress of Pericles, was said by Socrates to be the only person in Athens, man or woman, who could best him in argument. Phryne,

the model for the great sculptor Praxiteles, had achieved
a reputation for eroticism by bathing naked in the sea,
like the goddess Aphrodite, in the presence of numer-
ous admirers. Though all could not measure up to these
standards, the girls at the House of Selene were reputed
to be among the best in Alexandria. And Alexandria was
reputed to have the best *hetairai* in the Empire.

When Judge Severus entered the main room of the
house, he heard the sounds of courtesans practicing
flutes and stringed instruments and saw that everything
had been arranged according to the diagram in the case
file. There were seven couches set up around three sides
of a large low table. On each of the couches sat a woman
and a slave.

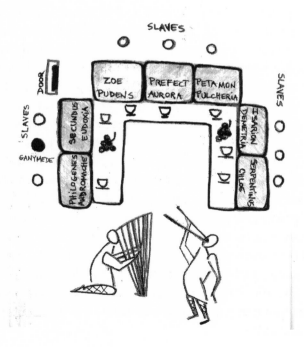

Each slave had a placard around his neck bearing the name of the orgiast he was supposed to represent. A young man with a silly grin sat on the couch in the middle of the long end of the table, opposite the open end, next to a stunning red haired woman with dark brown eyes in a red dress. He bore the placard that said "Prefect." On the "Prefect's" right, in the guest of honor's post, was the slave representing the victim, Titus Pudens, while the stand-in for Isis priest Petamon was to the Prefect's left. The short ends of the table had each two couches, with slaves representing Secundus and Philogenes on Pudens' right, and others with placards for the antique dealer Isarion and the Prefect's aide Serpentinus on Petamon's left.

Selene, the proprietress of the establishment, formally greeted Judge Severus and offered "every courtesy and cooperation with the authorities." She was an older woman, very beautiful, with her days as an active courtesan behind her. Her arms jangled with bracelets and her fingers were covered with rings. Her face had a determined, rigid expression as she showed the judge and his entourage -- Vulso and Flaccus -- to the chairs set up for them in front of the open end of the table.

Severus noticed that the walls of the room were decorated with painted frescoes, tastefully done, of nymphs and satyrs in suggestive poses. Any overtly obscene wall paintings, Severus knew, would be in the private rooms upstairs.

Three groups of slaves stood against the back and side walls, ready to serve food or drink. One of them bore the placard "Ganymede." He was placed in the group along the side near the door, behind Philogenes and Secundus.

"As you know," began the judge in Greek when he was seated and had taken in the scene, "I'm here to investigate the death of Titus Pudens. And I want to do it by recalling everything that happened the evening of the orgy, as far as your collective memories will take us."

The women nodded their understanding.

"Now," said Severus, "to begin with a few preliminaries. When was the party arranged, who arranged it, and who selected which *hetairai* were to attend and who they were to be paired with?"

"I can answer that," said Selene. The judge inclined his head to her. "The party was arranged by Secundus, the Prefect's stepson."

"When?"

"That morning. It was a little late, of course. Usually I require much more notice. But it was the Prefect of Egypt so naturally we did our best. The girls will remember that we were busy all day, rearranging our schedules, deciding what to wear and just getting ready."

"Had you serviced parties for the Prefect before?"

"Oh yes," answered Selene. "When was the last one, Aurora? About a month ago?"

The red haired woman in the red dress at the Prefect's couch agreed. "Yes, about then. There was some festival or other. The Prefect gave a large party."

"Were you at the Prefect's couch that time?" asked the judge.

"No. Not the last time. But at some previous parties, yes. He requested me again for himself at this one."

"That's right," chimed in Selene. "Secundus specifically mentioned that his stepfather wanted Aurora this time. The Prefect had Chloe the last time, right?"

"Yes," interjected a beautiful, slim, brown haired woman with green eyes. "But he had evidently finished with me." Her face took on a cynical look.

Selene quickly continued. "Secundus also chose his girl personally, when he came to make the arrangements." She nodded at the woman sitting with the slave with the placard 'Secundus.' Severus noticed that Secundus had chosen Eudoxia, a small young girl, almost boyish looking, but extremely attractive.

"I could select the others," continued Selene. "But he specifically said that Chloe was to go to Serpentinus this time and that there should be only one girl for each guest. At some past parties he had ordered two women for some of the guests, particularly for himself.

"He didn't give me a guest list, so I was hampered in selecting just the right girl for each guest. But," she swept her arm to encompass the assembled women, "you can see that any guest would be pleased with my selections."

There was no possible doubt about that, thought Severus.

"When we arrived at the Hadrianum, we were met by one of the Prefect's slaves and kept in a side room until we were called."

"When you entered," asked Severus looking at a tall blonde girl on the couch of the slave with the placard 'Pudens', how did you know which couch to go to?"

She answered. "My name is Zoe, *kyrie*. Aurora knew she was to go to the Prefect, Eudoxia to Secundus and Chloe to Serpentinus. But the rest of us went in and took any empty place or went with whoever motioned toward her. The men were, quite naturally, looking us over when we came in.

"I just happened to take the spot on Pudens' couch. He looked too frightened of us to be forward. I gathered that this sort of party was rather a new experience for him and I know I made him nervous. At least at first." She smiled ingratiatingly.

"How did he die?" asked the judge directly. "Did you see what happened?"

Zoe answered. "He had just had an orgasm and lay back on the couch. I took a clump of grapes from a bowl on the table and fed them to him, one by one. Then he stretched out his hand for a cup on the table. He just took the nearest one, or someone handed him a cup, I didn't really see, and he took a long drink. Then he gasped, clutched at his throat and went into a horrible spasm." She paled just recalling it. "I stood up and screamed and he half fell off the couch." The Prefect and a few others gathered around and examined him for life, but he was dead. The party then broke up."

"What about that cup he drank from? Try to remember again. Did he select that one deliberately or was it handed to him?"

"As I said, I don't know. I don't think even he glanced at it. He just reached out for a cup."

"Where was *his* cup?"

"Nearby. But apparently not as near as the one he ended up drinking from. They all looked pretty much alike. The same size, shape and color, but with different designs on the sides. One had a horse, another a dolphin, a third fruit, you know. The mix-up must have occurred during the brawl."

"What brawl?"

"When things started getting wild, when the revels began."

Aurora joined in. "After we came in, *kyrie*, we found our places, I began to sing a song. But it was obvious that most, if not all the men, were already quite drunk and weren't interested in music. They started shouting, yelling, making obscene gestures and then throwing things. Food, garlands and clothes were flying all over the place."

She looked at the girl on Isarion's couch. "Demetria was even chased around the couches. Isn't that right, Demetria?"

Demetria nodded. "That's right, *kyrie*. There was a grape fight between Secundus and Isarion. I think Secundus started it by throwing his garland across the table at us. Isarion then picked the grapes from a cluster and threw a whole handful at once at Secundus. He was shouting and laughing. That is, until Secundus hit him in the face with a whole cluster of grapes. Do you remember that, Eudoxia?"

The young girl on Secundus' couch recalled the incident. "Of course. I was the one who was hit by Isarion's barrage of grapes."

"Then," continued Demetria from Isarion's couch, "Isarion tried to shove a bunch of grapes in my face. I backed away and then he chased me around the couches.

"But he didn't catch me. When he circled behind the Prefect's couch, the Prefect tripped him. Isarion fell flat on his face and everyone burst out laughing."

"What were the other guests doing during the grape fight?" asked Severus. He looked at the girl on Philogenes' couch. "How did the Homeric scholar react to all this?"

The girl next to the slave placarded 'Philogenes' shrugged her shoulders. "I'm Andromache. He didn't participate in it. He seemed taken aback, actually. He was a very small man, but he tried to curl himself up and make himself smaller. Almost like he was trying to hide. He began to make some comment to me to show his distaste when a tunic came flying in our direction and knocked the wine cup out of my hand, spilling wine all over Philogenes."

"Who threw the tunic?" asked Severus.

"Secundus did," said Eudoxia. "He was standing on our couch, jumping up and own, and taking off his clothes and yelling drunkenly. He threw one garment in one direction and one in another. His tunic landed on Andromache's wine cup and his silk *synthesis* floated down in front of Pudens. Then he began to do an obscene dance, yelling for the musicians to play louder. He danced on the couch, on the table and on the floor."

"How did Pudens react?" Severus asked the blonde girl on the victim's couch.

"If Philogenes showed distaste," replied Zoe wryly, "then Pudens was almost in a state of shock. It was as if he couldn't believe his eyes at the goings-on. I don't think he was the sort that cared for a wild orgy. I took pity on him and began to caress him to calm him down. Then, I remember, I caught the Prefect's glance and he smiled and nodded as if to say I should continue what I was doing. I smiled back and did and Pudens submitted. I remember he kept his eyes shut during the whole thing."

"Aurora," asked the judge. "What did the Prefect do during all this, besides trip Isarion?"

"Well, he wasn't throwing things, but he was having a good time. He was laughing and making encouraging comments and generally participating. For instance, when Secundus was doing that dance on the table the Prefect was clapping time. He was also leaning back and forth, shouting comments to Pudens on his right and to the Isis priest on his left, encouraging them to join in the fun. I'm sure he was totally drunk. But then I didn't see everything. The Prefect pushed my head down to service him and I couldn't see what was happening."

"Did the Isis priest Petamon join in?" asked the judge of a beautiful, light-haired, dark-eyed girl on the couch to the left of the Prefect.

"My name is Pulcheria. No. The Isis priest just watched." She thought for a moment. "It wasn't that he was shocked or anything like that. He was just calmly reclining, watching everything with an amused smile. Then he excused himself to me and said it was necessary for him to leave the room. He had to make a ritual ablution before engaging in sex."

"And he walked out the door?" asked Severus, tracing the route with his eyes. It led from Petamon's couch behind the Prefect's, Pudens' and Secundus' couches.

"Yes, although he stopped briefly to whisper something into the Prefect's ear."

"Was the door in the Prefect's triclinium in the same position as the one in this room?"

"Yes," answered the girls in unison.

"How long was the priest gone?"

"Not too long," answered Pulcheria. "But I wasn't really paying attention. I was too busy trying to dodge flying objects." She laughed.

"What did Serpentinus do?" asked Severus to Chloe, the girl on the couch next to Isarion's, who had been with the Prefect at the previous party but had been given to Serpentinus by the Prefect this time.

"He was eating all the fish patties," she answered with a distasteful expression. "In fact, when Isarion was chasing Demetria around the room, he leaned over and stole their platter of fish patties. I wondered at the time how someone who eats like that could be as scrawny as he was. He looked like his name too, serpent-like, thin and creepy, with sunken eyes and sunken cheeks. And he treated me very roughly. He forced me down on the couch, held my arm in a painful grip and brutalized me from behind more than once. He was deliberately hurting me and my cries of pain stimulated him. I endured it with my eyes closed and stayed that way even after he finished with me. So I really didn't see much."

Severus turned to his assessor. "Flaccus, let me have the painting."

Flaccus opened a cylindrical box on his lap and extracted a rolled sheaf of papyrus. He handed it to the judge.

"This is a painting of the Prefect's slave Ganymede," said the judge as he unrolled it. He handed it first to Selene. "Please pass it among yourselves and tell me if you remember him from the party."

"Is he the slave who confessed?" asked Selene as she studied the painting.

Severus nodded. "Weren't you questioned about him?"

"Not really," she answered. "Secundus came by one day with some clerks and told us that one of the Prefect's slaves had confessed. He asked whether any of us had seen him do it. He didn't really question us like you're doing." She passed the painting to Chloe, the girl on Serpentinus' couch.

"I don't notice slaves," said Chloe with a touch of haughtiness as she looked at the painting, and then passed it to Demetria. Neither Demetria nor Pulcheria remembered him. Aurora, on the Prefect's couch, commented, "I remember some of the slaves, but not this one."

The girls on the Pudens and Secundus couches couldn't remember him either.

"It's beginning to look," commented the judge nervously, "as if he wasn't there at all."

"But I remember him," said Andromache from Philogenes' couch. "He was the one who refilled my wine glass after it was spilled by the flying tunic. And he was directing a young boy to wipe the wine off Philogenes and to clean up the floor."

"Are you sure?"

"Yes. I'm positive. It's him. It's a good likeness too."

"Did you drink the wine he poured into your cup?"

"Of course," she answered. "And I'm still here," she added, catching the judge's meaning.

Severus looked at the Prefect's couch. "Aurora, think again. Send her back the picture. Did Ganymede fill the Prefect's wine cup? The one with the dolphin on it. Or yours, perhaps?"

Aurora stared at the picture a long time. "I never noticed this person at all, and certainly not at our couch. Our couch was attended by two young slave-girls, who were stationed along the wall behind us. I think one was about 12-years-old and the other about 9 or so. I remember the child filled my cup and the older one attended the Prefect. They did it at past parties too."

"Did you and the Prefect drink from your cups after they were refilled?"

"Yes."

"Did no other slaves approach the Prefect's couch? Perhaps when sex was going on?"

"They wouldn't have dared," said several women at once. "And they couldn't have done it without being noticed," commented Andromache, "at least by the other slaves."

"What about the time that Secundus threw his clothes about. His tunic landed on Andromache on his right and his silk *synthesis* landed on Pudens' couch on his left. Is that right?"

"Yes," answered Eudoxia on Secundus' couch.

"That's right," joined in Zoe from Pudens' couch. "It must have been of a very fine gauzy material because it sort of floated down. It landed right at the edge of the table and the couch, covering some cups and half the food platters."

"Who removed it?" asked the judge, leaning forward in his chair.

No one could say.

"Ganymede?" asked Severus.

"Not very likely," said Andromache. "If he was servicing my couch with Philogenes, what would he be doing over at Pudens' or the Prefect's couches, on a different side of the table."

"And I don't remember him ever at my couch with Pudens," said Zoe. "Some of the other guests passed by at various times like Secundus or Petamon or Isarion or Serpentinus. I remember that, but none of the slaves that attended us were Ganymede."

"But not Philogenes," interjected Andromache, who had been on the same couch as the Homeric scholar. "He never left our couch at all."

"I agree," said Aurora. "At one time or another all the guests except Philogenes came to the Prefect's couch to say a word or two."

"So let me sum this up," said Severus, "and tell me if any of you disagree. Of the guests, everyone except Philogenes passed by the Prefect's couch. Of the slaves, they all stayed where they were assigned so only the two young girls were at the Prefect's couch. Ganymede only served the couches he was behind and was never at the Prefect's or Pudens' couch."

Severus looked at the *hetairai*, one after the other. No one disagreed.

"But then," said Selene, "if Ganymede never was at the Prefect's couch or at Pudens', how could he possibly have poisoned...?" She stopped in mid-sentence.

The girls all looked at each other quizzically.

Judge Severus didn't say a word. His face flashed a brief show of triumph and then he fought to contain rising anger. His fists clenched involuntarily. He rose from his chair, turned and stalked out.

IX

QUESTIONING THE
QUAESTIONARIUS
AND CONFRONTING SECUNDUS

There was just one more piece of evidence the judge was after. "If Ganymede was innocent," Severus put it to his staff, "why would he confess?"

"He was tortured," said Vulso. "He couldn't take it."

"Exactly," replied the judge with a wan smile. "So now we'll question his torturer."

Though most judicial torture was carried out in public as a salutary example of judicial authority and power to show the populace that the government was doing everything possible to solve crimes, there were also inside torture chambers for more secretive interrogations.

Severus and Flaccus descended the steps to the basement of the Hadrianum, where the inside judicial torture chamber was located. The court *quaestionarius* was waiting for them at the door. He was a short stocky man, with enormous shoulders, a neck like a bull, and the small red cap of his low profession on his head. He introduced himself as Rufus, opened the door with a key that hung from his belt and let them in the room.

As a judge, Severus was familiar with the arrangement. One part was the exact replica of a courtroom, with the Tribunal, a low platform for the magistrate, with three camp chairs on it; one for the judge, one for his assessor and one for the stenographer. On one side of the Tribunal was the statue of Jupiter Fidius, whose presence was necessary for an official Roman court, and on the other the court's water clock.

There was also a table for whips and another for medical equipment and a *furca*, a "Y" shaped wooden post to which the unfortunate victim was fastened during the inquiry.

"I have found in the court records, Rufus," began the judge directly, "that you applied the lash in the case of the Prefect's slave, Ganymede. Do you remember it?"

"Of course, *eminentissime*. He was the one who tried to kill the Prefect. It was an important case."

"I have discovered," continued Severus with authority, "that Ganymede was in fact innocent and that therefore his confession was false. I want to know how the examination was conducted. Did you hit him too hard or too often? Did someone direct you to conduct the session that way?"

"I just do my job, *eminentissime*," replied Rufus nervously. "But it's true what you say. Secundus did tell me to lay it into him. We'd been getting no results from the first few slaves, so Secundus told me to let this Ganymede really have it. I did and he confessed."

"Did he come right out with it? Or did Secundus suggest the answers to him?"

"Well, to tell the truth, it was a little of both. You know, Secundus would suggest something and then the slave would say yes, yes, and even added to it."

"Did you hit him a lot?" the judge asked grimly.

"Secundus told me when to do it," replied Rufus. He bowed his head. "To tell you the truth, *eminentissime*, I thought he told me to hit him much more than was necessary. The slave's back was a mass of blood and he was screaming horribly through it all. I knew it had reached the stage when he would say anything just to get me to stop. Even I sometimes have nightmares about it."

The judge turned around and walked out. Flaccus followed quietly behind him.

Before confronting Secundus, Severus made a quick stop in the law library to look up the exact wording of the law he had in mind. Then he headed to Secundus' office, where he found him talking to two clerks.

"Get out," said Severus to the clerks standing next to the young man. They took one look at the judge's face and hurried out, closing the door behind them.

"What's this all about?" asked Secundus, standing up slowly. He was frightened by the judge's manner.

"I have proof that the slave Ganymede did not attempt to kill the Prefect and that you tortured him so cruelly that he confessed to a crime he didn't commit." The judge began to excoriate him. He kept his voice under control but his manner was menacing. "There is no worse act of judicial injustice or incompetence than the one you have committed. You have procured false testimony to convict and condemn an innocent man. That's judicial murder. You're a disgrace and I mean to see that you answer for it."

A look of defiance had crept into the young man's eyes. "That slave was guilty. I don't know how much pain a..."

"Save your defense for the trial."

Secundus stopped short. "Trial? What trial?"

"Your trial," replied Severus, his eyes glaring. "For judicial murder under the *Lex Cornelia de sicariis et veneficiis* – the Cornelian Law on murderers and poisoners. The law specifically includes as liable, and I quote, "a magistrate presiding in a criminal case who renders a judgment based on false testimony by which an innocent person is convicted." That's what you did and I will instruct my court clerk to draw the charge sheet. You are to consider yourself under arrest."

Severus turned and opened the door, motioning for Secundus to go out. "You will go to your apartment in this building and stay in it until I hold a court session tomorrow morning. You may ask for bail at that time."

"This is absurd," shrieked Secundus. "There's not going to be any trial. Wait til my stepfather hears about this. I'm not going to my apartment. I'm going..."

"Vulso," yelled the judge into the hall. The Centurion strode in, accompanied by two armed marines from the quadrireme *Argo*.

"Vulso. Escort him to his apartment and place a guard at his door. He is not to leave it until called into court tomorrow. If he resists, use force."

Secundus stood motionless.

Severus walked up to him and slapped him in the face.

X

THE PREFECT GIVES HIS VERSION

The word of Secundus' arrest was all over the building in minutes. Within a half hour the Prefect was at Judge Severus' apartment in the Hadrianum.

"What's this all about?" he asked with a worried look as soon as he and the judge were alone.

Severus took the Prefect into the open air peristyle where they could enjoy the late afternoon breeze blowing off the sea. They strolled around the colonnade while Severus gave Calvus a brief explanation, reviewing the absence of corroboration for Ganymede's confession, the accounts of the women at the House of Selene exonerating Ganymede and the story of the court torturer indicating the use of excessive force to coerce a confession.

"I'm sorry," concluded Severus, stopping and facing the Prefect. "I know Secundus is your stepson, but I have been given full judicial authority by the Emperor himself, and I find myself in circumstances where the law compels me to use it. Your stepson appears to have committed judicial murder under the *Lex Cornelia*."

Severus paused. "Under our dual penalty system he doesn't face the death penalty because he's an Equestrian, and therefore an *honestior*, but exile or relegation to an island for life are possible."

Calvus sat down on a bench, bowed his head into his hands and stayed that way a long time. Then he looked up. "You know, Judge Severus, this puts me in a delicate position. On the one hand, I can understand that the young man may have been a bit over-eager, perhaps irresponsible, in his conduct of the investigation. But he is my stepson and I'm obligated to protect him. I owe that to his mother, may she rest in peace. You must expect me to exert every public effort in his behalf, though I hope you won't take it personally."

Severus nodded understandingly. The Prefect walked over to the lotus pool in the center of the peristyle.

"When Secundus first told me about Ganymede's confession, I found it a little hard to believe. Not, you understand, because I didn't observe him near the table -- I was, unfortunately, too drunk to remember anything. But I couldn't believe that Ganymede would do something so foolish as to try to kill me, even if he fancied that his wife and I were intimate. But I questioned him myself and he repeated his confession. I had no choice then but to allow the law to take its course."

"Prefect," replied Severus, "your position is even more delicate than you say. Because if Ganymede didn't poison your wine, then someone else did. And the person who did it has not been apprehended. He may make another attempt to kill you."

"I see," replied the Prefect. "What then do you suggest, Judge Severus?"

"First, I'm assigning a squad of marines from the ship that brought me here to serve as your personal bodyguard until we find the murderer."

"Really, judge, is this all necessary. I have a personal bodyguard headed by a former gladiator. He'll..."

Severus held up his hand. "It is necessary, Prefect. I'm responsible to the Emperor to see that you remain alive. I would be remiss in my duty if I failed to take such a simple precaution. Your bodyguard didn't prevent this attempt so I must insist on the increased protection."

The Prefect gave in with a shrug.

"Now, from the accounts of the women, it appears that at least ten people had an opportunity to reach your drinking cup. The Isis priest, Petamon, Isarion the antique dealer, your aide Serpentinus, Secundus, the two young slave girls who served your table, and the three *hetairai* at the head couches -- Aurora, the courtesan at your couch, Zoe the *hetaira* with Pudens and Pulcheria, the courtesan with Petamon. However Philogenes never left his couch, so he couldn't have done it."

"Secundus is also out," shot back Calvus. "Even if he doesn't honor me as his stepfather, he knows I am in the process of legally adopting him as my son. This will happen soon. So he certainly has no motive before then. Quite the contrary. He has a strong motive for keeping me alive.

"Also the slave girls are impossible. They are too young and innocent and are devoted to me. And they've had many other opportunities to serve me food and drink and haven't poisoned me. And the courtesans should also be eliminated. What motive could they have? Besides, if one of them had done it, she would hardly have provided evidence which clears Ganymede, and none of them implicated him."

"Then we can concentrate on either Petamon or Isarion or Serpentinus. Which of them would want you dead?"

The Prefect thought about it. "None of them. Just the opposite, actually. I can think of good reasons why they -- why all the guests at the party in fact -- would want to keep me alive."

"Why do you say that?"

"Take Isarion, for example. He's an antique dealer and I'm his best customer. Now it doesn't make any sense for him to kill me, does it?

"Or Serpentinus. He's my confidential aide and I pay him very well. My death would not be to his benefit at all."

"Or Petamon. I recently became an initiate into the Isis cult. Not only because it's good politics for the Prefect of Egypt, but also because I'm getting old and the Isis cult offers hope based on the wisdom of the ancients. Petamon is my teacher in the sacred lore of the Egyptians. Needless to say, his association with me has earned him a promotion in his Serapeum from 'Interpreter of Dreams' to 'Keeper of the Keys.' He's now next in line for 'Prophet' of his Serapeum and he knows if I am alive, I would see that he gets it."

"May I ask, Prefect, how Petamon became your teacher. Did you select him?"

"Secundus found him for me, actually. He had asked the 'High Priest of Alexandria and All Egypt' to find an appropriate priest to instruct me. The High Priest, despite his fancy title, is nothing more than the Roman official who oversees the Egyptian cult. His basic job is to descend unexpectedly on temple books and accounts. I believe Secundus said the High Priest spoke to the 'Prophet of the Great Serapeum' who selected Petamon.

"Petamon has proved to be very learned in sacred lore and can read the ancient hieroglyphics. I see him once every few days, whenever I get a chance to continue my studies in the ways of the Isis cult. He's a priest in the Serapeum outside the Moon Gate and I simply send a litter for him when I want him. We have gotten along well and I can't think of any reason why he would want to poison me."

"I see," replied Severus. "Still I would like to talk to him and the others. While no one may have personal animosity towards you, someone may have a political motive. After all, you are the Roman governor of this province and there are some opposed to Roman rule. And then there's a war on. Who knows who the Persian secret service has in their pay? The 'Eye of the Great King' is always dangerous to us."

"You can talk to Petamon any time, I suppose, since he's here in Alexandria, as is Isarion too, unless he's away collecting antiques. But Serpentinus is not now in Alexandria. He's away on a mission."

"What kind of mission, may I ask?"

"Actually I'm not quite sure. It's a mission for Secundus, so you'll have to ask him."

"Under the circumstances, perhaps you can ask Secundus and let me know that and when he'll be back."

Calvus nodded in agreement.

A slave appeared at the entrance curtain to the peristyle with a tray of refreshments. He poured some chilled white wine from a decanter and set two glasses on a low table next to the flower pool bench. He then retired as the two men sipped their wine.

"While we're on the subject," continued Severus. "I was wondering how Petamon came to attend your orgy. I thought priests of Isis are supposed to be celibate."

Calvus cleared his throat. "That's rather a recent development in the Isis clergy, Judge Severus. Not all the priests follow it. In the past, they were only required to remain pure prior to performing certain ceremonies. Brother Petamon observes those, of course. But there was, shall we say, nothing impending when he attended my little party."

"I see," said Severus, draining his glass. "Did you know, Prefect, that Philogenes has disappeared? He has been missing from his home and the Library for more than a week now."

"I didn't know that," replied the Prefect. "I've been wondering why I haven't seen him recently. He's a harmless Homeric scholar. I liked having him around because his literary knowledge impressed people. He liked to dance attendance on me, for the prestige I suppose. I send for him occasionally, particularly for parties. As I say, to impress people."

"Were you trying to impress someone the night of the orgy?"

Calvus smiled. "No. I invited him to this orgy as a reward for his services to me." The Prefect stood up and sauntered toward the doorway, indicating it was time to leave. "I hope nothing serious has happened to Philogenes. I expect he went on a trip. He tends to be absent-minded. He probably forgot to tell people he was going."

"Prefect, you seem to be exonerating everyone. But someone poisoned your drink. Who do you think it was?"

"I have no idea."

"Think harder. Your life may depend on it."

As they reached the front door to the apartments, Calvus returned to the subject of his stepson. "I hope you won't be too hard on poor Secundus. It's true that he sometimes tends to be rash, but he has by and large done a competent job on my staff, both here and in Rhodes, when I was Procurator there."

"I will certainly see," replied Severus obliquely, "that Secundus gets what he is entitled to."

The Prefect gave him fishy smile. "Then I will leave this whole matter in your capable hands, Judge Severus. In my next dispatch to the Emperor I must compliment him on his choice of emissary."

Severus thanked him and opened the front door. The Prefect's slaves lounging in the corridor immediately sprang to attention.

"There is one other thing," said Severus, "that I was wondering about. It's about Pudens, the unfortunate victim in all this. I noted from the diagram of the seating arrangements that he was placed on the couch on your right, the guest of honor's post. Was the party that night in his honor?"

"Not exactly. You see, Judge Severus, Pudens was an inspector in the Imperial Post. He had accompanied me from my office to my apartment as I was going home for the party. He was giving me some report or other about a matter he was handling. I don't even remember what it was about.

"But during his report, I was informed by messenger that one of the guests, the sub-Prefect, couldn't make it. An important matter had come up, requiring him to leave Alexandria. So on the spur of the moment I conceived the idea of inviting Pudens as a replacement. He was right there and an invitation would be an honor and reward for his capable service. He had been sent out from Rome years ago and served under three Prefects. Pudens, you may not be aware, was a total public servant; scrupulous and completely honest. A rare mixture in government, as I'm sure you know.

"He protested politely, of course, that he still had work to do that night, but I made him the guest-of-honor. He couldn't refuse."

Severus' face fell. "You mean that his attendance at the party was the result of a random series of chances? If he had waited until the next day to make his report, or if your guest had not cancelled out, or if you hadn't made that spur of the moment decision, or if there hadn't been a mix-up in the wine cups, Pudens would still be alive?"

Calvus nodded silently.

"It proves," concluded Severus with a wan smile, "the part the goddess Fortuna plays in our lives."

"There is no other explanation," agreed the Prefect.

XI

A LETTER TO THE EMPEROR

Marcus Flavius Severus to Marcus Aurelius Antoninus Augustus, Emperor. Greetings:

Domine, you asked me to keep you informed about the progress of my investigation into the attempt to kill the Prefect of Egypt.

Upon arrival I was informed by the Prefect that the person who put poison in his drinking cup had been found. He had confessed, was tried and had already been executed. It was a slave of the Prefect's named Ganymede, who supposedly harbored a suspicion that his wife had been unfaithful to him with the Prefect. Apparently the Prefect notified Rome that the culprit had been caught, but his letter did not arrive before I was already on my way to Egypt. You should have received his report by now.

However, in reviewing the file, I saw that Ganymede's confession was problematic. First, it was not corroborated, as Roman law requires, and second it was obtained as a result of judicial torture. I therefore sought to find corroboration. But what I have found instead is evidence that the slave Ganymede could not have been the person who put poison in the Prefect's cup. This comes from the *hetairai* who attended the party; they were all sure Ganymede was never anywhere near the Prefect's table. So not only is there is no proof of his guilt, but Ganymede appears to be innocent.

How was an innocent person executed? The Prefect's stepson Secundus was appointed special judge for the case, but violated the law in several ways. A Rescript of the Emperor Hadrian states that "slaves are to be tortured only when the accused is suspected and proof is first obtained by other evidence, so that only a confession is lacking." Here, Secundus ordered the random torture of slaves with no evidence implicating any of them.

A Rescript of Emperor Trajan states that under torture "the magistrate ought not directly to put the interrogation whether a particular person committed the crime, but he should ask in general terms who did it; for the other way seems to suggest an answer rather than to ask for one." Here, Secundus did not ask questions in a general way, but suggested the answers during torture.

In addition, it is the law that a "confession should not be considered proof of a crime if no other evidence is offered to corroborate it." This is because the Imperial Constitutions recognize that evidence obtained under torture is "weak and dangerous and inimical to the truth" because people often confess only to end the torture. Here, according to the *quaestionarius* Secundus ordered a degree of torture that even the torturer regarded as clearly excessive.

Secundus was therefore personally responsible for convicting and executing Ganymede on the basis of an uncorroborated false confession he obtained by directing the use of excessive torture. I have therefore charged the Prefect's stepson, Secundus, with judicial murder under the *Lex Cornelia*. His gross negligence or malice in this case was responsible for a horrible miscarriage of justice and the death of an innocent person.

Still, the question of who tried to kill the Prefect remains open. The Prefect told me that no one else at his party had any motive to kill him. Quite the contrary. They all thrived upon his favor and his death would only harm their prospects. This may or may not be so. I am therefore investigating whether any of them may harbor a hidden motive, perhaps a political one, for trying to kill the Prefect.

On the question of motive, we all know the famous words of the Consul Lucius Cassius Longinus Ravilla in the time of Republic. When sitting as a judge in a criminal case, he would always ask *cui bono*? -- to whose good? Who benefits? If no one at the Prefect's party would benefit from the death of the Prefect, it is only logical to ask whether someone would benefit from the death of the person actually killed – an inspector of the Imperial Post named Titus Pudens. Logic compels me to follow that trail as well. I will keep you informed.

Vale.

/Seal/ Marcus Flavius Severus.

XII

STRATON ATTENDS THE TEMPLE OF ISIS

The Serapeum outside the Moon Gate came to life just before dawn. For the Sun was about to rise and the most important priestly duty of the day was about to begin. Isis had to be awakened, washed, dressed and fed. Straton was right there at the entrance, before dawn, ready to join the early worshippers attending the ceremony. His ordinary looks, ordinary undyed tunic and sad brown eyes blended right in.

The program now was to learn about the people who attended the orgy, but surreptitiously. No need to alert them to the extent of Severus' interest or his methods. Straton had been assigned to Petamon, the Isis priest.

Straton entered the courtyard in front of the temple and joined the crowd around the fountain. He imitated them in performing ceremonial ablutions and then followed the worshippers entering the temple between the two huge statutes of erect phalluses. Inside, priests with shaven heads and clad in pure white linen robes welcomed the faithful with the traditional greeting, "May Osiris give you fresh water."

Straton entered just in time for the "Awakening of the Goddess". The doors to the sacred image of Isis were already opening when Straton squeezed through to stand near the front. While the congregation watched the statue with adoring eyes, Straton watched Petamon, the Keeper of the Keys, who had just opened the sanctuary door. He was roundish in shape, his bald head shone and he looked bored. No doubt, thought Straton, he would prefer to be at one of the Prefect's orgies. Straton watched him all through the singing of "Awake, Isis," but during the washing and dressing of the statue, Straton turned his attention to the other priests and priestesses busy with basin, towels, and the statue's garb of linen, jewels and vulture feathers. He was looking for someone with a friendly face and a dumb expression.

It took him most of the ceremony to find the one he wanted -- a young acolyte who shook a sistrum rattle during the lighting of the holy flame. Straton memorized his face. Then, while the priests were circulating through the congregation sprinkling them with the "cold water of Osiris," he extricated himself from the crowd and left the temple. He had decided to skip "the silent veneration."

There was a taverna across the way from the Serapeum compound from where Straton could watch the entrance while having breakfast. He ordered honey buns and red wine and settled at a table. Two hours and five honey buns later, the young priest who Straton was waiting for emerged from the temple carrying a sack and headed down the street. Straton followed him into a grocery, where the priest proceeded to fill his sack with cheese, olives and other supplies.

"May Osiris give you fresh water, brother," said Straton.

"May Osiris give you fresh water, brother," answered the priest in a friendly manner.

Straton selected some olives from a large vat and put them on a piece of papyrus. "I saw you at the service this morning," he said chattily. "You played the sistrum."

"That's right," answered the priest with a smile. "Are you a regular worshipper at our Serapeum?"

"I'm a devotee of the cult, but I'm new in Alexandria. I come from Corinth where I attended the local Serapeum regularly. Now that I'm here, I'm looking for a Serapeum to attend. Everyone I ask suggests a different one and there are forty-two in the city, I hear."

"Yes. It's a difficult choice. But perhaps now that you've seen our service, you might choose us. Do you live nearby?"

"Not far," answered Straton. He appeared to think of something. "Have a drink with me, brother, and tell me about your Serapeum. You're right. I was greatly impressed with the service. Maybe I should join."

The priest seemed pleased. "There's a taverna just around the corner," he said, and led Straton to it.

They sat down and Straton ordered Egyptian beer for them both. A vat was placed on the floor with two long reed straws sticking out of it. The priest sucked up a portion of the brew and Straton imitated him. The beer was bitter, but he could taste the sweetening honey mixed in.

"We don't get this in Corinth. It's refreshing."

The priest sucked up some more and said his name was Psen-Mon.

"Have you been a priest long?"

"I'm an initiate," answered Psen-Mon. "I'm not yet on the second level, but then I've only been here for two years."

"How many priests are in your Serapeum?"

"Fifteen."

"Ah," said Straton. "That's the perfect number. In Corinth there was one Serapeum with too few and another with too many. But yours is just right."

"And," continued Psen-Mon, "our Prophet, Isidorus, is very learned in the sacred rituals. He is also very good to us."

"I noticed the Keeper of the Keys when he opened the door to the statue. He also looks very learned."

"His name is Petamon," informed the priest, becoming excited. "And do you know he instructs the Prefect of Egypt in the ways of our cult."

"He does?" said Straton with a show of great interest. "You mean the Prefect is a member of your Serapeum?"

"It's not generally known yet, but it's true. Our Serapeum is most honored by it and Petamon has risen from Interpreter of Dreams to Keeper of Keys in the shortest possible time because of it."

"How long was he Interpreter of Dreams?"

Psen-Mon looked a little doubtful. "I don't know. He only came to us last year. But he was Interpreter of Dreams for many years in a Serapeum in Rhodes."

"Rhodes?" said Straton, ordering a bowl of chickpeas for the table. "I've been there. I'm a mosaicist, you know. I travel frequently for special jobs. I do very fine work. That's why I'm in Alexandria."

A slave-waitress brought the chickpeas, half flinging the bowl across the table.

"Was your Keeper of Keys in the Serapeum near the ruins of the Colossus?" asked Straton, figuring there would be one somewhere near the famous fallen statue. "That's the one I used to attend."

The priest thought for a moment, trying to recall what he had heard. "I really don't know." Psen-Mon sipped some beer. "Were you in Rhodes when they had the scandal?" he asked Straton in a manner suggesting that "the scandal" was common knowledge among followers of the Isis cult.

"Yes," replied Straton quickly. "Wasn't that terrible? What did you think of it?"

"We all think the government was too harsh in crucifying the priest. He only let the Inner Sanctuary be used for the escapade. But he didn't take any part in it himself."

"I agree completely," encouraged Straton.

"After all, it's not as if he was the one who dressed up as the god Anubis. They didn't do anything to him."

"It's unfair," said Straton, commiserating.

"It's only because the lady was wealthy and a Roman."

"Is it true that she wasn't even beautiful?"

"Yes. That's true. I know someone who once saw her and he said she wasn't even beautiful. What else did you hear about it?"

"Nothing else, except that if she wasn't beautiful, how could she expect the god to want to sleep with her. So the whole story is probably untrue. They executed our priest for something that probably never happened."

"That's what everyone was saying in Rhodes too. But you can't argue with the government. You know the Romans."

The priest finished his beer, rose and lifted up his sack. "I'd better be getting back. I've been away too long already. I hope, brother, that you'll join our Serapeum and that I'll see you again. It's been a pleasant conversation."

"I will join. You convinced me."

"May Osiris give you fresh water, brother," said Psen-Mon.

"May Osiris give you fresh water, brother," replied Straton.

XIII

ARTEMISIA VISITS
AN ANTIQUE SHOP

Artemisia took a breath, thought of a rich Roman matron with a passion for spending money, and let herself be helped down from the litter. Her assignment was to find out about Isarion, the antiques dealer who had attended the orgy. But at his shop "The Golden Ibis" she learned that he was away on the island of Rhodes. So after browsing a short time, she went to a nearby shop, "The Falcon of Ptah." Its owner, Tkutis, she had been told, was one of Isarion's chief competitors in Alexandria's antiques market.

For her impersonation, Artemisia was dressed in an expensive Roman style *palla* of Chinese silk and her hair was swept up in a complicated coiffure sprinkled with gold dust. She sported a pearl in her hair comb and jewels blazed from rings on her fingers. A young slave, rented along with the fancy litter, opened the door of the antiques shop of "The Falcon of Ptah" and Artemisia breezed in, accompanied by her own young slave Galatea and her husband's slave Glykon, attending her on this little expedition.

The slave boy in the shop took one look at what was coming in the door and ran into the back to get the proprietor as quickly as possible.

Tkutis appeared almost instantly. He was very small, not quite a midget, but not much bigger and he bowed so low and so fast that he looked like a puppet. His eyes shone as brightly as the coins he was already counting. He barked out a few commands in Egyptian and slaves appeared from the back hauling out cushions, wine and fruit for the rich Roman lady.

Artemisia swept her hand in a broad gesture, encompassing all the cases and shelves and tables of ancient glass, jewelry, statuary and antiques. "I'm interested," she announced, "in everything."

Though her Greek was pure Athenian, having been born and grown up in Athens, at the antique store she deliberately spoke Greek with a Latin accent. Artemisia was very good at this mimicry, usually done for laughs among friends, but now it was for dissimulation.

For the next half-hour a parade of antiquities passed in front of her for review. The proprietor, introduced himself as the owner Tkutis, and played his customer expertly, emphasizing the beauty, rarity and genuineness of the expensive pieces, without downgrading all his other merchandise. There were many items from ancient Egypt, from the time of the pharaohs, he stressed. In a smooth and subtle manner, Tkutis spun stories and anecdotes about his wares, enhancing the desirability of owning them. Some statutes were said to possess special powers, some glassware had been drunk out of by a pharaoh himself. "The great Sesostris," he assured, "was reputed to have this cup with him on his expedition to Ethiopia, 2,000 years ago." His boxes had once kept magical potions for the high priests of long ago and were still, it was said, imbued with their spirits.

Tkutis tested his customer's knowledge. He passed off good, but not his best, wares at his best ware prices, until he saw that the Roman lady was more discerning than she first appeared. When she insisted on his best items, he took her to the room upstairs. It was obvious at a glance to Artemisia that here were his best antiques. Tkutis simply raised his prices, while complimenting his customer's acumen and commiserating with her on the high price of really good antiquities.

At the end of an hour, Artemisia and Tkutis sat on opposite ends of a table in the upstairs room with a few of the store's most expensive items between them. They were bargaining over prices, where Artemisia was not proving as tough a customer as she did over the quality of the merchandise. But that was deliberate. Artemisia was also playing Tkutis.

"You know," she said when she appeared almost to have decided to buy at a very high price, "I must be truthful with you. Yours is not the first antiques store I've been in on my tour of Egypt. This morning I went to the "Golden Ibis", the store of Isarion. You must know him. His shop is nearby. He was recommended to me by the Prefect of Egypt himself."

Tkutis held up his hand. "Of course I know Isarion, great lady. I know all the antiques dealers in Alexandria. It is my business."

"As I said, I was at Isarion's before I came here and I saw a number of beautiful items there." She described several antiques similar to the ones on the table, saying she had seen them at Isarion's shop earlier that day. "I would buy them all, yours and his, if I had my way, but my husband, you understand..." She let the sentence lapse when Tkutis looked sympathetic.

"Isarion wasn't at his shop this morning. They said he was away on business, so I didn't meet him. I always like to talk to the dealer personally. I believe I can tell a lot about the genuineness of the antiques by the genuineness of the dealer. Don't you agree?"

"I do indeed, *domina*," clucked Tkutis. "There are so many fakes on the market these days. So many antique dealers are unscrupulous."

"So," concluded Artemisia, "it's really a question of comparing your beautiful antiques with his. My husband might let me buy one collection, but not two." She took up a gold inlaid blue scarab with hieroglyphic writing from the table and fingered it admiringly. "Perhaps, Tkutis, you can tell me something about Isarion and his reliability as a dealer. I feel I can trust you to be truthful."

Tkutis smiled and rubbed his hands together. He looked almost gleeful. He was going to enjoy smearing a competitor.

"*Domina*," he began, "if you wish to judge Isarion's wares by the character of the dealer, let me tell you a little story about Isarion. You can ask any other merchant. They will tell you the same thing."

She looked at him expectantly.

"*Domina*, it grieves me to say this, but not all of Isarion's antiques are genuine."

"No. It can't be true. I don't believe it."

"It is true. Last year a boy who said he was from one of the villages along the Nile near Thebes came to Alexandria and made the round of antique shops. He had with him several items he said were found in the fields by the tombs of the pharaohs. He had many beautiful items with him. Gold cups, ancient jewelry, inlaid boxes, all of a very ancient and valued style. And he was successful in selling them to some of the antique dealers in Alexandria. One of the dealers, however, who has a very discerning eye, became suspicious of the genuineness of the articles the boy was showing around. A rumor began circulating -- I don't know where it started -- that the items the boy was selling were fakes. Not really old Egyptian pieces, but rather expert copies made in a workshop near Alexandria.

"This dealer -- the one who became suspicious -- decided to do a little investigating. He had the boy followed secretly and he discovered that the boy was having frequent meetings at night at the home of Isarion.

"A few months later the boy showed up again, this time with a new batch of alleged antiques. Again the dealer had him followed, and again he was seen to meet secretly with Isarion. Then another dealer, who was going up-country, agreed to inquire at the village the boy said he came from. When he returned from his trip he told some of the merchants that the villagers had never heard of this boy, nor had they heard of any antiques recently found in the area. So all the dealers stopped buying from the boy. All, that is, except Isarion, who continued to sell pieces similar to the ones the boy offered around. In fact, Isarion seemed to have an endless supply of these antiques.

"In short, *domina*, it is the consensus of antique dealers in Alexandria that Isarion is knowingly selling fakes and may even be the one who is behind their production. Unfortunately, there was little we merchants could do.

We would try to run Isarion out of the market place, but many government officials buy from him and he knows them well. They would protect him."

"But you could tell them about Isarion," suggested Artemisia, "that he is selling them fakes."

"He would say we're backbiting. Because he has the best Roman trade and not us. And honestly, *domina*, it is sometimes hard even for an expert to tell the real from the expert fake. He would say he is right and we are wrong."

"How do I know, Tkutis, that you are not saying these things about Isarion just to get his business?"

Tkutis shrugged. "Either he is a fraud or I am. You have talked to me and can form an opinion. You have seen my wares. Am I a fraud?"

Artemisia smiled at him. "No, Tkutis. I don't believe you are."

She was dissimulating but she bought five small blue faiance scarabs with gold hieroglyphic writing, one for herself, one for her husband and one for each of her children. Each had hieroglyphs for the Egyptian words "*ankh, wedja, seneb*" – life, prosperity, health. It was once a formula for pharaohs; now it was for Roman tourists.

XIV

FLACCUS AND PROCULUS ASK QUESTIONS AT THE IMPERIAL POST

For Flaccus and Proculus, their assignment was to find out what they could about the victim, the Imperial Post inspector Titus Pudens.

They found the offices of the *cursus publicus* -- the Imperial Post -- without any trouble, first because it was located in the Broucheion, the Greek and Roman area of the city, not far from the Prefect's residence, and second because it was next door to stables of horses and mules, carriages and chariots. The smell of these animals and their loud snorting and stomping as well as the chatter of their caretakers gave away their location.

Flaccus and Proculus were both dressed in Roman togas. They entered the office and announced themselves and their authority as aides of the imperial emissary, Marcus Flavius Severus, and asked to talk to the person who now had the job Pudens held before his death. Having notified the Imperial Post of their visit ahead of time, they were immediately escorted by a slave into the presence of an official named Archelaus. He was a thin little man with a tired, overworked and stressed look. He had a twitch on the right side of his face that every now and then distorted his right eye and the right part of his mouth. His right hand noticeably shook.

"We're here to ask you about the person who preceded you in this job, Titus Pudens."

"Yes, poor man. What a tragedy. To die like that, by mistake and so suddenly. But life is uncertain."

"What was his job exactly? What is your job now?"

"My job, his job, was as an inspector to see that the Imperial Post is functioning as it should. You know, of course, that the *cursus publicus* is a government institution, run by the government, for government business. It is not a private postal or delivery service. Only people with a special *diploma* issued by the Emperor, or here in Egypt by the Prefect of Egypt, can use it. Only government mail, government supplies, government reports and travelers on government business can use it. My job, Pudens' job, was to make sure that only authorized use is being made of our facilities and to investigate and stop any abuses."

"And what was Pudens investigating at the time of his death?" interjected Proculus.

"I don't know. I wasn't his assistant. I'm newly assigned here from up country, from Memphis."

"Who assigned you then?"

"The Prefect. Or should I say his special assistant, Secundus. I never actually met the Prefect. But Secundus tapped me for the job, for the promotion, saying it was because I had done such a good job in Memphis."

"We would like to speak to Pudens' staff then," said Flaccus.

"You mean his assistant Claudius Celer?"

"I suppose that's the person we want."

"He's not here. He was transferred back to the Imperial Post office in Rome, where he came from."

"Who transferred him and when was he transferred?"

"Secundus had him transferred. After Pudens' death. Or so I'm told. It was just before I arrived. But office gossip is that he wasn't officially transferred back to Rome; he fled there on the first ship out."

"Is there anyone else who knows what he was working on?"

"Not that I know of. Apparently Secundus reorganized the whole office."

Flaccus and Proculus then surveyed everyone else in the office -- clerks, stable hands, even slaves -- about the possibility that Celer fled rather than being transferred. But the consensus was clear. The official story was that he was transferred; the unofficial that he fled. No one had any first hand knowledge; it was all rumor and gossip.

When Flaccus and Proculus reported back to Severus, the judge was both alerted and dismayed. Alerted if Pudens' assistant had been sent away by Secundus. Even more alarmed if he had fled. That would imply that Celer feared Pudens' death meant he himself was in danger. But that was just rumor.

The judge was also dismayed because once again he felt stymied when there was someone he wanted to talk to who was no longer available.

"There are three people who attended the orgy that I haven't been able to talk to. Philogenes, the Homeric scholar and librarian, is missing. Isarion, the antique dealer, is in Rhodes and Serpentinus, the Prefect's aide, is on some sort of secret mission for Secundus. Then the wife of the wrongly executed slave Ganymede was sent to Italy. Now Pudens' assistant is no longer here, either deliberately transferred out or scared off. Something is wrong. As the saying goes, 'where there is smoke, flames are close by.' And there is too much smoke around here."

XV

SEVERUS SPENDS THE DAY AT THE MUSEUM OF ALEXANDRIA

While Straton was at the temple of Isis pursuing Petamon and Artemisia was at the antique store of Tkutis pursuing Isarion, and while Flaccus and Proculus were at the Imperial Post pursuing Pudens, Severus took a break from his duties and went to the Museum of Alexandria – the house of the Muses – pursuing his interest in astronomy.

The Museum was the institute for higher learning where the world's great scholars were supported by stipends in their study and investigations of Nature, of mathematics, of history, of literature, of the arts and of other intellectual subjects. They resided and worked together at the Museum and exchanged ideas to advance the cause of knowledge. The Great Library had first been established as an adjunct of the Museum.

The Museum's astronomical researches and persons working there were legendary, both in the fields of mathematical astronomy and observational astronomy. Euclid himself had been at the Museum, as had been

Archimedes, Aristarchos, Hipparchos, Eratosthenes and currently Claudius Ptolemaeus. These great astronomers had through geometry, mathematics and observations accurately measured the circumference of the Earth and the distance to the Moon. Other measurements, like the distances to the Sun, planets and stars were less well known, if known at all, but subjects of ongoing investigation and active study.

Severus couldn't get to see Claudius Ptolemaeus, the current doyen of astronomy. He was now over 80 years old and not seeing visitors much any more. But the Prefect's office had set up an appointment with one of the chief mathematical astronomers, Leonidas of Sicyon, and a tour of the astronomy facilities.

Leonidas was tall and thin and personable, with a stylish short white beard and an equally stylish white Greek tunic with red geometric designs. But he doubted that this eminent Roman visitor was anything more than a dabbler in astronomy.

"Are you able to understand a technical book on astronomy like this one?" he asked doubtfully, displaying a scroll full of geometry and mathematical calculations.

"Possibly," answered Severus without hesitation. "When I was a student in Athens I didn't study only with Stoics and Epicureans, but also with an eminent Platonist. And we all know the famous motto Plato had inscribed on the façade of the old Academy – 'let no one enter who does not know geometry.' Even though that building doesn't exist anymore, many Platonists, including my professor, still insist on geometry as a requirement. So I studied it and was good at it and still study it in my spare time. I can certainly understand something of that book, though I would have to study it."

"So you got some real benefit from your studies in Athens," replied Leonidas, somewhat mollified.

"And not just in the field of astronomy," added Severus, "but personally too. My wife is the daughter of that professor of Platonism."

"Let me show you our astronomical instruments first." Leonidas took Severus up to the roof where were set up a variety of astronomical devices for observing and measuring the heavens. There was a large gnomon or sun dial to measure time. Then there was an astrolabe, for measuring positions of the Sun, Moon, stars and planets and for making calculations. There was also an armillary sphere, a sort of spherical astrolabe consisting of a spherical framework of rings, centered on the Earth, that represented celestial longitude and latitude. Then he was shown a large diopter, which was a long rod with an occlusion device and a sliding scale for focusing on astronomical bodies. Severus mentioned that he himself had a small personal diopter he used on some nights for his own observations of the sky. There was also a *scaphe*, a new type of sun dial invented by Aristarchus with a pointer on the inside of a hemisphere marked off with angles and an equatorial ring for measuring equinox points when the shadow of sun fell on the ring itself. There were several public *scaphe* rings in Alexandria, including a large one in a major square, but this one at the Museum was the finest.

After the interesting tour of the instruments, Severus was invited to join a few members of the astronomy department for lunch in the Museum's eating hall. There he got to discuss astronomical subjects with the experts. He was introduced to one astronomer from Carthage, another dressed in oriental garb from Babylon, and a third,

who he was told was a young genius in mathematical astronomy, Timon of Ephesus. Timon was thin and gaunt,
dressed in a plain brown tunic with food stains and had
an unkempt appearance. He immediately lapsed into
some sort of reverie while everyone else started eating
the plentiful and excellent stuffed grape leaves, olives
and fish cakes. Chilled white wine was placed on the
table to drink.

The discussion turned to unsolved questions in astronomy about which there was much disagreement.
Questions like does the Earth stand still and the Heavens
move or the Heavens stand still and the Earth move? Is
the Universe finite or infinite? What were the nature of
the planets and stars? How far away were they? Were
the heavenly bodies inhabited? Which is the most distant planet?

"That one can be answered with confidence," piped
up Timon in a soft voice, suddenly coming out of his reverie. "Saturn is the furthest away. We know that because
it takes Saturn the longest to get back to any fixed position in the sky. For instance, if you look at Mars tonight,
you will see it in the constellation Leo the Lion, near the
star Regulus. Other nights throughout the year it will
have moved and will appear in other constellations. But
it will be back in Leo near Regulus in about two years.
Jupiter will reappear in any particular location again after 15 years, but Saturn takes 30 years to get back to the
same place in a particular constellation. The conclusion
is clear. The circuit of Saturn is longest because it is furthest away from Earth. And Jupiter is further away than
Mars, but closer than Saturn."

And so the discussions continued throughout the
lunch between Severus, who was knowledgeable and

could ask interesting questions, make relevant comments and express intelligent opinions and the Museum astronomers who were even more knowledgeable. They contributed to Severus' stimulation and enlightenment.

Towards the end of the luncheon the subject of Roman astronomers came up and Severus offered the story of Gaius Sulpicius Gallus. Gallus had been a military Tribune with the legions before the battle of Pydna against the Macedonians 300 years before. "Gallus was not only an officer but an astronomer and he asked to address the troops before the battle, because as an astronomer he knew there would be an eclipse of the Moon the following night between the 2nd and the 4th hour. So he explained to the soldiers what was going to happen, telling them it was just a natural phenomenon, predictable and no more ominous than the Sun rising and setting or the phases of the Moon.

"When the eclipse occurred, the Roman soldiers were ready for it and thought Gallus possessed great wisdom. The Macedonian king and his soldiers, however, were spooked and demoralized and thought it was an omen of the fall of their kingdom. Their soothsayers were equally confounded and they lost the battle.

"Later, in retirement, Gallus spent his time charting and measuring the Heavens. 'How often the rising Sun surprised him at his work at night', reports Cicero, 'how often the night came upon him when working on his charts during the day'."

The astronomers all smiled in appreciation of the story of a fellow astronomer. But in fact they had all heard it before, and from practically every Roman visitor to the astronomy department. Still, polite indulgence was the appropriate response.

After lunch Severus was shown an exhibit of mechanical and pneumatic novelties by one of the Museum's greatest inventors – Heron of Alexandria. Many of them seemed quaint, like a contraption that turned rapidly on the power of steam or another that made use of a wind wheel to operate a musical organ. There were also a variety of coin operated devices. One dispensed water when a coin was inserted into a slot, dropped onto an pan inside which tilted and opened a valve letting out water until the coin fell off the pan, closing the valve and shutting off the water. There was also a mechanical force pump invented by Heron that was already in use in the city of Rome and elsewhere for pumping water to put out fires.

Later that night, Severus was invited to join an observation session on the roof, tracking and observing the planet Mars and various stars. He felt at the same time the satisfaction of an accomplished astronomer and the awe of a little child.

When he left the Museum, he also felt he had one of the best and most memorable days of his life.

XVI

ALEXANDER DEVISES A PLAN TO FIND THE MISSING BOOKS

Alexander had devised a clever plan to trace the books missing from the Great Library. He told it to Judge Severus before the court hearing on Secundus' indictment. They were in temporary chambers attached to one of the Hadrianum's courtrooms, where Severus, Flaccus and Proculus were doing some last minute paperwork on the charge sheet and the accompanying legal documents.

"It's quite simple, really," said Alexander. "I think we should buy the books back."

Severus looked at him with a quizzical smile. "It's a good idea, Alexander, but just how are you going to find the person who now has the books in order to buy it from him?"

"That's my idea. I think we should induce him to find us."

Flaccus and Proculus stopped their joint proof reading of a document and came over when they heard the gist of Alexander's remarks.

"Whatever would make him come to us?" asked Flaccus.

"Money," replied Alexander. "Lots of it. I think we should offer the best price for the books."

"Perhaps you have something there," remarked Severus. "We could use a front man working for us, perhaps a book dealer would be willing to help. He could spread the word around the bookshops that he's interested and willing to pay a huge price. It might reach the right ears."

"It would sound suspicious," ventured Flaccus. "The thief might suspect a trap."

"Not if we did it right," interjected Alexander quickly.

"I see Alexander has something more in mind," commented Severus. "What's your idea?"

Alexander pulled out a sheet of papyrus with the names of the four stolen books, the Callimachus book of poetry, the first volume of an early edition of Homer's *Iliad*, the philosophic work by Lycon of Tarentum and the Hebrew book, *The Wisdom of Ben Sira*. He pointed at the last one on the list.

"Anyone might be interested in the first three, but the last one is mostly valuable to Jews. What I propose is that we find someone in Alexandria's Jewish community to buy it back for us. Then the thief wouldn't be suspicious of the purchaser or the price. He would head straight for it."

Severus started to smile. "Who do you have in mind?"

"I thought," Alexander answered nonchalantly, "we might try the scholar who was translating the book into Greek for the Great Library. His name, I found out, is Manassah ben Jacob and he lives in the Delta section of the city, near the Sun Gate."

Severus eyed his secretary narrowly. "Have you already spoken to him?"

Alexander nodded in a positive gesture. "I took the liberty of sounding him out yesterday."

"What did he say?"

"He was eager to do it. He says the book is a treasure for the Jewish community in Alexandria. He would be glad to cooperate in any attempt to buy it back. He said he could spread the word through the book dealers that the Jews know the book has been stolen and they want it back. They would pay a good price, with no questions asked. He wanted only to talk to the Ethnarch of the Jews in Alexandria before committing himself, but he was sure the Ethnarch would agree.

"I told him that I could supply the money, as well as surveillance and protection for him. I said we wanted the thief. The Library would get the book back. I also told him that I would have to consult with someone before I could finally authorize it."

"How much does he think we'll have to offer to buy it back?"

"Perhaps 2,000 sesterces. Manassah says that would be a very good price."

"It may already be sold," cautioned Severus.

"We know. But Manassah doubts it. Who would buy it but Jews and he hasn't heard of it being bought. So he thinks it's worth trying."

Severus turned to his clerk. "How much is our draft on the provincial treasury good for?"

"A lot more than that," answered Proculus.

Severus headed for the door to the courtroom. "Tell him to offer 5,000."

XVII

SECUNDUS IS GRANTED
BAIL AND FOLLOWED

The court hearing was brief. The defendant Secundus was ushered in and informed of the charges against him. His lawyer was handed a copy of the charge sheet accusing Secundus of judicial murder under the *Lex Cornelia*. Then the lawyer made an application for bail, arguing that there were sureties waiting to put up the money and his client hadn't confessed. Judge Severus set a moderate amount for bail and scheduled a trial date in ten days. Secundus' face bore a sullen impenetrable mask throughout the proceedings.

When it was over, the judge returned to his chambers and Secundus returned to his apartment. A half-hour later Vulso reported to the judge that Secundus had packed a bag and left the Hadrianum.

"Where do you think he'll go?" asked Severus idly.

"I don't know. But wherever he goes, he'll be followed closely. I have a squad of marines from the *Argo* assigned to him. He'll be covered like a blanket," concluded the Centurion with a grin.

It wasn't long before the first messenger from the surveillance team arrived. Secundus had taken a litter from the Hadrianum to a square near the Moon Gate. From there he walked two streets to a two-story apartment building and entered it. A short while later he emerged with two men, one a young man of decidedly foppish appearance and the other apparently the slave of the first. They had gone into a grocery and bought a large amount of food and carried it back to the apartment. Discreet inquiry in the neighborhood had ascertained that the young man was a Greek named Cupid and the other was Eumolpus, Cupid's slave. Secundus, the report concluded, appeared to have shacked up with a male lover.

"Have Cupid followed also," was the judge's reaction. "And if all three leave together again, sneak in and search the apartment."

Severus and Artemisia decided to take a walk that evening after dinner and enjoy the street scenes of Alexandria. Vulso accompanied them, for the judge had decided to walk in the direction of the apartment house where Secundus was ensconced. He would just check on the surveillance and walk back to the Hadrianum before dark. Both the judge and his wife were dressed in light summer evening tunics of Greek style.

By the time they left, the streets weren't crowded since most people were home having dinner, Greeks traditionally eating later than Romans. The smells of food cooking on countless apartment house braziers wafted out into the cool air, joining the aromas from taverns, restaurants and cookshops which were all crowded. Frying fish and freshly baked bread delighted the air.

Most of the stores were still open. There were a few fancy processions of wealthy people in litters on their way to dinner parties. Small crowds gathered here and there around a street poet or auctioneer. Severus and Artemisia stopped for a while to listen to a street musician play a beautifully mysterious oriental melody on an Egyptian harp. He told them the melody was his own composition and they asked him to play it again, which he did. They gave him a silver coin when he finished and ambled on.

Artemisia inspected a few stores on a street of leather merchants and they stopped into a shop selling inlaid Egyptian wood boxes. The boxes were so beautiful, the workmanship so admirable and the price so reasonable that Artemisia bought several for presents to take back home. One had a geometric design in ebony and ivory, another an inlaid winged Sun, surrounded by an Egyptian border pattern of little squares of red, yellow, blue and green, repeated around the central design.

After about an hour they reached the surveillance post. Vulso directed them to a taverna around the corner from the target apartment house where Secundus was staying. The taverna bore a signpost with an obelisk. Then he signaled to a man down the street, who signaled to someone else. Moments later, a man dressed in an ordinary brown tunic came over and said something to Vulso. Vulso brought him to the taverna to meet Judge Severus.

The surveilling marine told the judge that discreet inquiry had determined the apartment Secundus and Cupid occupied was on the second floor. The only thing that happened, recounted the marine, was that about an hour ago the slave boy left hurriedly carrying a message tablet. "One of our men followed him to the area around the Moon Gate, but then lost him in the crowd. The slave returned to the apartment a short while ago, still carrying a message tablet. Now we're waiting."

A few moments later Cupid walked out of the building and turned left down the street. He turned the corner and walked on the sidewalk right in front of the taverna where the judge, his wife and four marines were talking. Severus got a good look at him when he passed by. He was a thin young man, with a mincing feminine step, wearing an effeminate long-sleeved silk tunic. His face was made up with powder and gold dust covered his hair like dandruff. He pranced down the street without even a glance in either direction.

Severus rose from the table. He motioned to Artemisia and Vulso. "Come on, let's follow him."

Vulso tried to dissuade him. "There are already two men on him, judge. It's a tricky job to follow someone without giving yourself away."

"Don't worry, Vulso," said Severus, pulling the Centurion out the entrance, "he seems completely oblivious to everyone on the street and with the way he's dressed we don't have to worry about him melting into a crowd."

Cupid headed into the Egyptian quarter, walking toward the Moon Gate. He paid no attention to the shops beginning to close down or the late shoppers making quick purchases and hurrying home. He never looked behind him. The judge, Artemisia and Vulso hung back about three quarters of a street behind Cupid and had no trouble keeping him in sight.

After a quarter of an hour walk, Cupid entered a taverna that bore a signpost with the name and a painting

of "The Two Crocodiles." Vulso ushered Severus and
Artemisia into a shop two doors up and across the street
from the taverna. They couldn't see inside.

"Let the marines handle it now," cautioned Vulso.
"One of our men just followed him inside. The other is
outside."

They proceeded to browse among the wares of the
shop they were in, mostly copperware – plates, bowls
-- while keeping an eye on the tavern entrance. Vulso
brushed aside the proprietor with an abrupt instruction
to be let alone. He backed away from them and resumed
his seat at a table in the rear, where he stroked the sleeping store cat.

A few minutes later a man in an ordinary worker's
tunic approached Vulso, whispered something into his
ear, and returned to a post from where he could watch
the tavern's interior. Vulso conveyed the message to
Severus.

"He went into a room in the back of the taverna.
There's a curtain in front and we don't know what or
who is behind it."

Severus nodded and resumed inspecting the copperware. A few other customers walked into the store and
the proprietor attended to them. It was now dark outside
and people on the street were now carrying lanterns or
torches to light their way. The tavern entrance was lit
dimly by the light from oil lamps inside, but anyone entering or leaving could be seen from Severus' vantage
point in the shop. When the other customers had left, the
proprietor asked them to leave because he had to close
the shop. Vulso told him that it would be impossible,
they were there on a police matter. The proprietor returned to his table and played with the cat.

A few minutes later a signal from the outside agent
alerted them that Cupid was coming out. He appeared at
the door, barely glancing at the street, and headed back
in the direction he had come from. A marine followed
him. Vulso received a signal from the other marine.

"Another person has come out of the curtained
room," he told Severus. "Look, he's at the entrance now
and walking this way."

Severus watched him stroll by the shop. He was
a bald-headed man dressed in a long white linen robe,
tightly drawn around the chest and descending almost to
his feet, which were shod with white palm leaf sandals.
An Egyptian priest.

"I'll bet," whispered Artemisia to her husband and
Vulso, "that the priest is Petamon."

"Have him followed," Severus instructed the
Centurion.

"There's no need to have him followed," countered
Vulso. He pointed down the street. "Look who's coming out of the taverna."

Severus watched a familiar man look up the street after the priest and stroll along behind him. "I guess there's
no doubt about the priest being Petamon," laughed the
judge. "After all, who else would Straton be following."

Later that night, Straton reported to Judge Severus
that he had followed Petamon from the Isis temple to
"The Two Crocodiles" tavern, where he went inside and
disappeared behind a curtain. After a while a thin, foppish young man with gold dust all over his hair and wearing a long-sleeved tunic – "Cupid" interjected Severus –
came into the taverna and disappeared behind the same
curtain. After a while Petamon came out and left the

taverna. Straton was unable to get close enough to hear what went on behind the curtain.

"So why was Petamon meeting Cupid?" asked Vulso, knowing the answer even as he asked the question.

"Evidently Cupid was there to deliver a message from Secundus to Petamon or to take a message from Petamon to Secundus."

"Or both," continued Vulso.

"Or both," agreed Severus.

XVIII

CUPID'S APARTMENT IS SEARCHED

A t the 3rd hour the next morning, Vulso checked in at the observation post in the "Obelisk Tavern" across from the apartment house where Secundus was holed up. He spoke to the marine in charge of the surveillance team. Secundus and Cupid had left an hour ago, reported the tough looking marine. They were walking arm and arm and looked like they were going out for a day on the town.

"What about the slave?" asked Vulso.

"He's down the street shopping for pots."

"How long has he been there?"

"Not long."

"Delay the slave," commanded Vulso animatedly. "I'm going in."

"How should I delay him?"

Vulso thought a moment. "Offer to buy him a drink. And if he's so impolite as to refuse, knock him cold."

Vulso ran up the stairs to the second floor and found the door of the apartment. He knelt down and studied the lock. Then he reached into a pouch on his belt and extracted his lock picks. It was only an ordinary lock and it took Vulso only the ordinary amount of time to spring it. He straightened up, opened the door and walked in.

The room was large and fancily decorated with expensive colored silk hangings and an obscene wall mural showing a variety of orgiastic scenes involving combinations of men, women and mythological creatures. The room smelled of attar of roses and a variety of antiques decorated shelves and tables. Vulso went to a door leading to a hallway. There were rooms on either side. One, sparsely furnished, was obviously the slave's, while the other was lavishly decorated. It featured a gilded bed with coverlets of fine Chinese silk and a mattress that reeked of perfume. There was a table with papers and writing equipment against one wall. Against the other wall, on the floor, were two chests. Next to one was the musette bag which Secundus had brought with him from the Hadrianum. Vulso went for it, opened it up and peered in. It was empty. He tried the lid of the chest next to the bag. It opened. A pile of tunics was laid neatly on top on one side, and a variety of toiletry articles was on the other. Vulso took out the clothes and carefully placed them on the bed.

Underneath was a collection of papyri. He unrolled the top sheet and read it. It was a copy of the criminal charge sheet in Secundus' case. There were also other documents which looked like copies of the file in the case against Ganymede. Vulso saw Ganymede's confession to putting poison in the Prefect's cup and the statement Secundus had obtained from the sorceress Phna, denying she had sold poison to Ganymede. There was nothing else of interest. He walked over to the table and examined the papyri on it. One looked like it was being worked on. It was an unfinished document, written on good quality papyrus in black ink, with many editing marks and crossings out in red ink. Blank spaces were left to be filled in later. A sheaf of the same quality papyrus was on the left and a writing case with red and black inks on the right. Vulso picked up the papyrus and read it.

"Year 3 of the Emperors Marcus Aurelius and Lucius Verus, in the Prefecture of Marcus Annius Calvus, year 2, the ...day before the... of....

"To the Court of the Prefect of Egypt, from Philogenes, scholar at the Great Library of Alexandria.

"I make this affidavit as a witness in the case against the slave Ganymede. I declare that I saw the slave Ganymede pour wine into the Prefect's dolphin cup. I also saw..."

It was unfinished. Vulso smiled to himself. Not only hadn't Secundus figured out the date of the affidavit but he hadn't yet decided what else Philogenes had seen.

The Centurion sat down at a desk, pulled a fresh sheet of papyrus from a pile, and made a copy of the document, even duplicating the red editing marks. Judge Severus would undoubtedly be pleased to have a copy, he thought while writing. He could place it under court seal that day and have it opened if Secundus tried to present a finished version in court. It would bury him.

Vulso finished the copy, cleaned the pens, replaced the tunics in the chest and left the apartment. He was careful to relock the door with his tools. He walked down the stairs thinking about what made Secundus so confident his fabricated affidavit would not be contradicted by

Philogenes. Did he know the Homeric scholar was dead and could never repudiate a forged signature? Or did he know Philogenes was alive and would sign it?

When Vulso came out he saw the two marines squatting on the sidewalk playing dice.

"Where's Cupid's slave? I thought you were buying him a drink?"

The tough looking marine got up from the game. "If you go around the corner and walk down the street, you'll see a crowd of people gathered around a street-corner doctor."

"Yes?" said Vulso, a malicious grin coming to his face.

"That doctor," continued the marine," is setting someone's fractured ribs." The marine returned his own malicious grin. "Those ribs belong to Cupid's slave. You see, sir, he refused to have a drink with me."

XIX

THE PAULINA AFFAIR

The trumpets blared, the drums beat and the sema-
phore signal flags waved. Judge Severus stood on
the ramparts of the legionary camp at Nikopolis. It was
near noon and the Sun was scorching the plain below,
while a wind whipped up along the battlements. The
Prefect of Egypt, other toga-clad high government officials, and a crowd of uniformed army officers lined the
ramparts, watching the Legion II Traiana Fortis maneuver on the plain below.

Ten cohorts, each of 360 soldiers, formed separate
solid squares on the plain. The first line of four cohorts,
with three open spaces between them, advanced in battle
formation, javelins ready, their long oblong shields up,
swords in scabbards slung at their sides. Skirmishers
of light cavalry wheeled on the flanks, while slingers
and archers screened the advance. The second line of
three cohorts, arranged behind and between the spaces
in the front line, followed closely behind, while a third
line of three more cohorts brought up the rear. The order
to charge was given. Spears were thrown. The roared

battle cry of almost 4,000 men called "*Vae Victrix*" -- "Woe to the Vanquished" -- and the standard bearers leaped forward, followed by the whole legion. The Sun flashed off the metal armor and helmets of the troops, as if a blazing, flashing bronze and silver river were in motion, while the dust of the plain arose around the advancing war machine.

"They're keeping formation nicely," Severus heard an army officer standing next to him comment to an aide.

The Legate in command of the legion, observing from the ramparts, gave an order and a semaphore-man signaled the troops below. The trumpets sounded in response and the frontal attack turned into an oblique maneuver, with the left wing holding back in a defensive position as a pivot, while the right and center advanced, the right rapidly and the center more slowly -- like a door slamming shut.

Severus stared fascinated at the spectacle. He had never seen anything like it. There was an incredible feeling of power and force emanating from the advancing army. The jumbled noises and movements of ferocious men and spirited horses and clanking armor made the ground shake and the air vibrate.

The commander waited until the right wing had pivoted 180 degrees and then halted the whole legion now in line facing the opposite direction. "They're out of line," screamed the Legate at his staff. "The center was too slow. The Persian cavalry could have ridden through that gap and taken us in the rear." The Tribune who was being yelled at went pale. "Get down there," yelled the Legate, "and see that they do it right this time." The Tribune and his staff scrambled down the stairs.

The observers relaxed and took wine from platters that army orderlies were passing around. The Prefect extracted himself from his staff and headed toward Judge Severus.

"I'm sorry to have dragged you all the way out here," Calvus apologized, "but I hope the spectacle is worth it."

"It certainly is," replied Severus.

"You can also report directly to the Emperor when you return to Rome about the battle-readiness of the II Traiana Fortis. These drills are the heart and soul of the army. You know what they say about the legions – 'their drills are like bloodless battles and their battles are like bloody drills'. But that, I'm sure, is not what you wanted to talk to me about."

"No. I wanted a few minutes of your time to ask you about an incident that occurred in Rhodes recently, perhaps while you were the Procurator there."

The Prefect looked at him expectantly.

"I have some information about a scandal which occurred in one of the Isis temple's there, involving a priest of Isis who was executed for his part..."

"The Paulina Affair," interrupted Calvus. "Yes. I know it well. Being the Procurator of the island, I presided at the trial. What is it you want to know about the affair?"

"I want to know all about it."

"Does it have to do with the attempt on my life?"

"It may."

"Let's walk along the rampart where it's less crowded and I'll tell you the story."

They strolled to another side of the tower. Two army officers talking there saw the Prefect and moved away. Calvus and Severus had the whole side rampart to themselves. They leaned on the balustrade and peered down at the walls, courtyard, barracks, hospital and administrative buildings of the army base. The wind had died down.

"The affair involved a superstitious and gullible Roman matron, a young man who had conceived a passion for her, and a priest in one of the Isis temples in Rhodes. Curiously, what happened here mirrored a scandal many years ago in Rome during the reign of Tiberius. Perhaps the culprits here read about it in Tacitus and were inspired by it.

"At any rate, Paulina was a woman of noble Roman ancestry and had a reputation for virtue. Though she was young and beautiful and might have led a flirtatious life, she instead led one of great modesty. Her husband was Saturninus, a member of the Senatorial Class, and he was on an Imperial Commission sent out from Rome to Rhodes to inspect public works projects. He too had an excellent character and together with Paulina they lived exemplary lives.

"As fate would have it, unfortunately, a young man named Decius Mundus, a Roman Equestrian, conceived a passion for Paulina and began to send her presents and pay visits to her when her husband wasn't home. She rejected all his advances, but this only inflamed Mundus' passion. He became so infatuated with Paulina that he went to her home and offered her 200,000 drachmas to enjoy her once. When she indignantly refused and ordered him from her house, he was not able to bear it and decided to starve himself to death.

"Now, Mundus had a freedwoman named Ide, who was always up to various sorts of mischief. She heard about what happened and went to Mundus while he was starving himself and encouraged him to take heart, for she had a plan whereby he could enjoy Paulina. Her price was 50,000 drachmas. When Mundus heard the plan he agreed and Ide carried out her part. She was a member of the Isis cult and she knew Paulina as someone very much devoted to the worship of the goddess Isis. So she went to one of the Isis priests who was her friend and offered him 25,000 drachmas to help in the seduction of Paulina. For that much money, he agreed and he went to Paulina's home.

"The priest told Paulina that he had been sent by the god Anubis, who had fallen in love with her because of her noble character and sincere religious beliefs. The god had bidden him, the priest alleged, to visit Paulina and invite her to sup and sleep with Anubis in the inner sanctuary of the temple. Paulina was flattered by the message from the god and boasted to her friends about this epiphany of the god. She also told her husband about it and after much discussion he agreed that she could accept the offer, being fully confident of his wife's chastity and the holiness of Anubis."

The Prefect wore an amused smile on his face as he told the story.

"So Paulina went to the temple and after dining in the inner sanctuary with the priest, they waited until the hour to go to sleep. Then the priest closed the doors of the temple, put out the lights in the inner sanctuary and left.

"When he had gone, Mundus, who had been hiding there all along, leapt out, dressed in the costume of Anubis, complete with a jackal-head mask. He proceeded to enjoy Paulina and kept her at his service throughout the night, indulging in every form of sex act he could imagine. He left the next morning, before the other priests in the temple awoke.

"Paulina went home and told her husband about the visitation. She also boasted about it to her friends. Many were skeptical, considering the nature of the incident, but others, when they considered her modesty and merit, saw no reason to disbelieve her.

"On the third day after the incident, however, Mundus and Paulina chanced to pass each other on the street and Mundus, who was in very good cheer, couldn't resist the temptation to say something. So he told Paulina that she had saved him 200,000 drachmas, yet had not failed to be at his service. When she asked what he meant, he joked that Mundus was unconcerned about her reproaches as long as she continued to love Anubis. He then tried to make another appointment with her.

"Naturally, the woman was quite distraught. She went home and tore her clothes and finally brought herself to tell her husband, begging him to help her. Saturninus was furious and brought the matter to my attention, as Procurator. I had the matter investigated. Secundus was in charge of it, as a matter of fact. He had the priest arrested, of course. The priest confessed and implicated Ide. Then Mundus was also arrested. I found the three of them guilty and sentenced the priest and Ide to be crucified. Mundus, being of Roman *honestior* status, was entitled under the law to a lesser punishment and I sentenced him to five years banishment. And after all, his crime was out of love, not malice. I should also add that when the legal research for the trial was done, we found that case involving a Serapeum in Rome during the reign of Tiberius. I followed precedent and my verdict was the same as Tiberius' -- exile for the young Roman man and execution for the foreigner priest. Tiberius also demolished the Serapeum and had the statue of Isis thrown into the Tiber, but I didn't feel called upon to do that. I just closed that Serapeum."

The Prefect began to walk back to the side of the tower facing the plain, for his staff was calling to him. The maneuvers were about to resume.

"I hope I've answered your question, Judge Severus, though I'm curious about what the Paulina Affair has to do with the attempt on my life."

"Did you know, Prefect, that Petamon had recently been a priest of Isis in Rhodes?"

"At the Serapeum where the Paulina Affair occurred?" asked the Prefect with surprise.

"I don't know that yet. But it might provide a motive of revenge for Petamon on behalf of the Isis cult. Perhaps he felt the priest was unjustly executed by you."

"I can hardly believe that's the case. But Petamon never mentioned he had been in Rhodes, though, I suppose the subject never came up between us. Do you think the whole Isis cult has it in for me? Maybe I should suspend my instruction in it for a while."

"That might be a good idea. However, perhaps you could send your litter for him once more tomorrow. I'll talk to him about it."

A member of the Prefect's staff importuned him to resume his place on the ramparts so the maneuvers could continue.

"I have one more quick request," said Severus hurriedly. "I also have unearthed some information that the antique dealer Isarion may be engaged in selling fake antiques."

"What?" reacted the Prefect. "That's not possible. I buy from him myself and all my pieces are genuine. I know. I'm a connoisseur. Where'd you hear such malicious gossip. From other antique dealers?"

Severus nodded. "It may be only a rumor. But I would like to get an independent expert's opinion of the items you've bought from Isarion. Just to be safe."

"That's ridiculous, Judge Severus. I know him well. But if it will satisfy you, I'll have those pieces looked at."

He turned and headed toward the center of the reviewing stand. The signal man waved a colored banner and the trumpets blared on the plain.

The great war machine flashed and roared into motion.

XX

JUDGE SEVERUS INTERVIEWS THE PRIEST OF ISIS

Severus had given some thought about how to conduct the interview with Petamon. Should he wear a toga and be imperious -- try to overwhelm him? Or should he wear a tunic and be casual -- try to draw him out? Should it be in judicial chambers or in the gardens? Which would best strip the priest of his defenses and get him to react? Severus finally decided on a combination -- a toga and chambers for a display of authority and a friendly manner. Perhaps he would insinuate that Petamon was himself to blame for poisoning the Prefect's cup at the orgy or, if not, that he might know who did it or suspect someone else. Then he would see what would happen, who Petamon might accuse, for instance. Or he could challenge him about the Paulina affair. In any event, he would see how the interview developed, just like gladiators were told to "take counsel of the arena".

Petamon didn't show any reaction when he was brought to see Judge Severus rather than the Prefect. But he became wary when Severus explained that Ganymede was innocent, that he was charged by the Emperor to conduct his own investigation into the attempt to kill the Prefect, and that he was naturally interested in interviewing everyone who attended the orgy.

"I hope you don't think that I had anything..." countered Petamon defensively.

Severus held up an open palm. "Of course not, Petamon." He said it with an expression on his face and a tone in his voice that made his denial deliberately unconvincing. "But my first thought was that since Secundus cruelly tortured Ganymede into confessing, it was possible that Secundus did it to cover his own crime. How does that strike you?"

"Secundus?" said Petamon weakly. Severus smiled at him. "Oh no, *kyrie*. It couldn't have been Secundus. I'm sure of that."

"Why?"

"Because Secundus is going to be adopted as the Prefect's son. That couldn't go forward if anything happened to his stepfather. He could therefore have no motive."

"I see," said Severus. "But do you know Secundus' character? Perhaps he is a malicious person. Perhaps he is self-destructive. Or maybe he wants to inherit the Prefect's money as his stepson, even before adoption. Is Secundus in debt?"

Petamon didn't know exactly how to answer that. He took out a handkerchief and mopped his brow. He looked around as if to see what was making it suddenly hot in the room. That he was beginning to sweat did not escape Severus' notice.

"I know Secundus is not like that."

"Really? How well do you know him?"

"Not really well," answered the priest quickly. "I naturally met him because he is always with the Prefect and I formed a good opinion of him. But I haven't talked to him much."

"Do you have any contact at all with Secundus other than at the Prefect's parties?"

"No. Only there."

Evidently Petamon was not going to mention his meeting with Cupid, who had come to meet him straight from Secundus, only a few days before at "The Two Crocodiles" tavern. And Severus had no intention of letting Petamon know that he knew about it.

"What about Secundus' reputation? Perhaps you have talked to people who know him and commented on his character?"

Petamon wiped his brow again. Beads of sweat were already standing out quite clearly on his bald head as well as his brow. He waved his arm vaguely. "I don't really know about Secundus, *kyrie*. But he would have no motive. I know that."

"Then if it wasn't Secundus who tried to kill the Prefect, who was it? Who do you suggest?"

"I don't know anything about crime, *kyrie*. I'm sure I couldn't tell you..."

"Isarion, perhaps? Do you know him?"

"No...I...Yes, I've met him. I met them all, except Pudens. They are friends of the Prefect. There were other parties I attended. They all seemed of exemplary character. I can't answer your question."

"Serpentinus too? Did you meet him before?"

"Serpentinus? Oh, you mean that aide of the Prefect. No. I don't think so. Maybe I did. I'm not sure."

"You didn't know him in Rhodes by any chance?"

"In Rhodes?" The priest mopped his brow again and twisted the handkerchief between his hands. "I don't think so. Maybe. I don't know."

Severus sensed that Petamon had been sufficiently unnerved. "Where were you during the Paulina Affair?" He asked it with a cold edge to his voice.

"I had nothing to do with that," he snapped back.

"I didn't say you did," replied Severus casually. "I just asked where you were. Was that your Serapeum?"

Petamon hesitated. Severus thought he was deciding whether to lie or tell the truth. He opted for the truth.

"Yes. It was my Serapeum. And I knew the priest who was crucified. I..." He stopped. The train of Severus' inquiry became clear to him.

"If you think, *kyrie*, that I tried to kill the Prefect because he was the judge in the Paulina Affair..." He couldn't complete the sentence.

Severus stared at him menacingly. "The thought had occurred to me."

"I want to see the Prefect. He can tell you this is absurd. Take me to him. I didn't try to kill him."

"The Prefect is too busy to see you. In fact, the Prefect will continue to be too busy to see you until this matter is cleared up."

"This is outrageous." Petamon was about to lose his temper.

Severus squashed him. "You're forgetting yourself, priest. I'm the personal emissary of the Emperor of Rome. You're a mere priest of a foreign cult. You will act accordingly. That means you will answer my questions, not characterize them. Is that clear?"

"Yes, *kyrie*," he replied meekly.

"Now," continued Severus, "go to that table in the corner with papyrus, pen, and inkwell and write an account of everything that happened at the Prefect's orgy, as you remember it. I want a detailed account of what everyone did, who left their couches, who was near the Prefect's couch. Everything. I have already spoken to the courtesans who were there and I have their statements. So yours better be the truth.

"Then, after you finish that, I want a written account of everything you know about the Paulina Affair."

"But I can't remember such..."

"Write what you remember," commanded Severus standing up. "When you're finished, tell the guard to call me."

The judge opened the door and left the room. An armed marine in full uniform came in, closed the door behind him, and stood guard against it.

"What did he write?" asked Artemisia later that night.

Severus handed her the papyrus that Petamon had written.

"Drivel. He claims a failure of memory. He says he was drunk. He doesn't remember anyone leaving their couch during the party."

"Not even himself, when he went to make pre-sex ablutions?"

"He doesn't mention it."

"Or Secundus' dance on his couch?"

"He doesn't mention that either."

"That's not much help."

"On the contrary," corrected Severus. "I now have his affidavit in writing. That means he can't come forward at the trial of Secundus with any story that he saw Ganymede do it."

"I see," said Artemisia laughing. "Very neat."

XXI

CLIMBING THE LIGHTHOUSE

In the three days following Severus' interview with Petamon, there was some progress. Severus prepared for Secundus' trial and listened to the reports of his aides. Straton had succeeded in worming his way into the Moon Gate Serapeum as a devotee and with the help of the young initiate Psen-Mon, had met some of the other priests. Two of them had been in the Rhodes Serapeum at the time of the Paulina Affair and Straton was working on teasing information out of them.

A report from the Prefect said that an expert had confirmed the antiquities he purchased from Isarion were all genuine.

Vulso reported that Secundus and Cupid had, for the most part, remained together in Cupid's apartment. One night, two girls had gone there and stayed until the next morning.

Severus and Artemisia took a day to go to the Pharos Lighthouse and climb to the top. First, with other tourists, they boarded a wagon which took them up a ramp to an entrance part-way up the first stage – the square almost

300 foot high base. Then they climbed up inside, stopping here and there to peer out the slitted windows. At the top of this level there was an observation deck with a great view and food vendors with snacks and drinks. Severus and Artemisia concentrated on the view, walking around the octagonal base of the next stage enjoying the magnificent, breathtaking scene – the sea on one side, the city on the other. Though most tourists stopped at this stage, some with aching thighs and dizzy from the height, it was only a start for Severus and Artemisia who were determined to go on and up to the fire chamber and reflecting mirror.

The second stage was the octagonal 100 foot tower where they entered and ascended a spiral ramp, along with a few tourists and carts carrying up wood to feed the flame at the top. But at the top of the octagonal tower there was another observation deck. Now almost 400 feet high, 4 times as high as the 10-story *insula* of Felicula in Rome, they were buffeted about by even stronger winds than below, and were even more amazed by the magnificent panoramic view of the gleaming white city and the sparkling blue-green sea. They could even see to the south past the city to the Nile delta and Egypt itself.

Artemisia flung her arms out wide, with her feet wide apart, and her head tilted upward to the Sun, feeling the wind and smiling into the sky. Then she threw her arms about her husband, whispering into his ear, "If there were no other people around, I would throw off all my clothes and make love to you right here." Severus put his arms around her and melted in her embrace.

But there was still one more level to go; the third 100-foot tower, circular in shape, leading to the fire chamber and mirror on top. After resting for a bit, they looked up, nodded to each other and went up, this time up a stair case surrounding a central shaft where a lift system could convey firewood on palettes to the top. When they finally made it to the top, they were tired and out of breath, but invigorated from completing the climb. Once again they admired the view, now from almost 500 feet up. Here they were almost giddy from the height, even a little scared from the narrowness of the top chamber, but they were still enthralled. They had never been so high.

Now they walked around the huge bronze mirror that reflected the central fire 30 miles out to sea at night. The guide on top told the tourists stories that the curved mirror had the property of magnifying objects in the distance and sometimes they could see across the Mediterranean to the city of Byzantium in Europe. But, said the guide ruefully, the weather won't permit it today. That left most of the tourists skeptical because the weather was perfect.

After the long climb down, Severus hired a two-person litter to take them back to their apartment in the Hadrianum. They first fell asleep in the litter and then, reaching their apartment, collapsed into bed without having dinner and slept until the middle of the night. Then they awoke, remembered being high in the middle of the sky, threw open the shutters of their bedroom to allow in as much wind as possible, threw off their bed clothes, and made love excitedly, passionately and several times.

In the following days they recovered and attended the theater, one Greek play and one musical performance of citharists, and then spent two evenings in the suburb of Canopus, enjoying the pleasures of a pleasure city with the crowds of carefree Alexandrians seeking a good time. They were attended by their slaves, Glykon and Galatea, on these evenings until at one point Severus noticed both slaves were not in sight.

"Where are they?" he asked his wife.

She smiled at him. "I told them they could go off by themselves and have a good time in Canopus. You may not have noticed but they've become lovers ever since we arrived here."

Severus smiled back and put his arm around her. "The magic of Egypt!"

"Yes, my *deliciae*, the magic of Egypt!"

On the third day, Artemisia had her own schedule – a special tour of places associated with the life of Cleopatra. An historian from the Museum guided her through the old palace by the harbor that Cleopatra used 200 years before to the place where the queen and Marcus Antonius were buried side by side. The guide told her about Cleopatra and Antonius together, about how they played dice together, hunted and fished together, went incognito into the streets of Alexandria at night together and named themselves and the group of companions in their flamboyant life style the 'Inimitable Livers.' At the palace Artemisia was shown the dining hall where Cleopatra on a bet famously dissolved a priceless pearl earring in vinegar and drank it. And where the food she and Antonius had at their banquets was cooked to perfection, always ready to serve at a moment's notice. How did the cooks manage this? the guide asked rhetorically. If they were having roast boar, they had eight boars roasting in the kitchen, all at different stages, so that whenever Cleopatra and her guests were ready, so would be one of the boars. She was also a gifted linguist, mentioned the guide, speaking 9 or 10 languages, including

Greek, Latin, Egyptian, Aramaic, Hebrew, Parthian and Ethiopian.

"What a woman"! exclaimed Artemisia admiringly.

"Perhaps too wild and uncontrollable," replied the guide.

"What a woman"! repeated Artemisia.

That night, when Severus and Artemisia returned from their evening stroll, Alexander was waiting with a message. Severus had rarely seen him so excited.

"It's from Manassah ben Jacob," said Alexander. "The Jewish scholar who is helping us find the missing books. They made contact."

"Excellent," said Severus. "Who with?"

"Manassah had told a book seller he knows about the interest of the Jewish community in getting the Hebrew book back. The bookseller spread the word around and has received what he thinks is a serious feeler. The thieves, he says, want 10,000 sesterces in Roman gold coins. That's 100 gold aurei."

"Good," replied Severus. "We have them on the hook. Tell Manassah not to overdo it. The price doesn't matter. Tell him to arrange a meeting."

XXII

ALEXANDER AND MANASSAH BEN JACOB BUY A BOOK

Two days later negotiations between intermediaries were completed and final arrangements made for the purchase of the stolen Hebrew book, *The Wisdom of Ben Sira*. The price was 10,000 sesterces, paid in 100 gold Roman aurei. The sellers had designated a place for the exchange as the back room of the taverna in the Egyptian section called "The Two Crocodiles". The time was to be the 8th hour of the day, early afternoon.

"That's the same taverna where Petamon and Cupid met," observed Severus. "Alexander, you go with Manassah to the meeting. I'll requisition the money from the provincial treasury and Vulso will take a squad of marines from the *Argo* to surround the neighborhood and arrest whoever you meet after the transfer."

At the appointed hour Manassah ben Jacob and Alexander entered the taverna and asked a slave-waiter for the back room. Manassah was tall and wiry and dressed in a long robe of Judaean design; Alexander was in a simple brown tunic under a plain cloak. The place was fairly crowded, with belly dancers and musicians going full blast. The slave pointed to a beaded curtain and the two men walked through it. No one was there. They sat down at the only table and waited. Alexander pulled his cloak tightly around him and felt the two pouches uncomfortably dangling from his belt. Each pouch contained 50 gold aurei. No one came to take an order for drinks. A half hour passed.

"Maybe they're not coming," ventured Manassah.

They continued to wait.

A short time later the curtain parted and two men entered. They were also wearing cloaks, with hoods covering their heads, obscuring a good view of their faces. One was a thin, wiry man, while the cloak couldn't obscure the size and bulk of the other. He looked like a gladiator or wrestler from his size and bearing. The thin man sat down, while the huge one positioned himself against the wall and watched.

"Do you have the money?" the thin man asked. His voice was edgy.

Manassah nodded. "Do you have the book?"

The other nodded in response. "Let's see the money first."

Manassah nodded to Alexander who withdrew the pouches from his belt and put them on the table. The man grabbed for the first one, emptied it and smiled as he ran his fingers through the gold coins. He then reached inside his cloak and pulled out a cylindrical case, from which he extracted a scroll. He shoved it across the table to Manassah and reached for the second pouch and looked inside.

Manassah mumbled a quick prayer in Hebrew and opened the scroll, scanning it rapidly. "It's the one we want," he said to Alexander and got up to go.

The large man came over and gently pushed Manassah and Alexander back into their seats. "We'll leave first," said the thin man, "just as soon as I finish counting the money."

He poured coins out of the second pouch, counted them all, put the gold back into the pouches, closed both pouches and then rose. "You two will wait here another hour."

Manassah and Alexander sat still.

The two men then went through the curtain, through the tavern and out the front entrance. They walked right into the arms of Vulso and the squad of marines from the *Argo*.

"You're under arrest," said Vulso, as the squad drew their swords and surrounded them, pushing them against a wall. Some of the marines kept the crowd back, while others searched the two captives, quickly retrieving the pouches of gold coins.

"What's this all about," the thin man screeched. "Leave those bags alone. They're mine."

Vulso grabbed him roughly. "Where'd you get that book?"

"What book?" he answered defiantly. "I don't know what you're talking about."

Manassah and Alexander came out of the tavern with one of the marines. "That's them," said Alexander. "I have the book," said Manassah.

"Where'd you get it?" repeated Vulso.

"I never saw these two before," replied the thin man.

Vulso gave him an evil grin. The thin man saw it and imperceptibly pressed himself against the wall, away from the Centurion.

Vulso swiftly turned him around, drew his hands behind his back and handcuffed him. Then he punched him in the small of the back. The man screamed. Vulso grabbed a clump of his hair and dragged him down the street, while the marines cleared a path.

"Stop it," yelled Vulso's captive. "You're hurting me. Let me go."

Vulso passed a grocery, a carpet shop, another wine shop and then stopped with his prisoner in front of a blacksmith's stall.

"By the order of the Emperor," said Vulso to the blacksmith, "I need the use of your shop."

The blacksmith took in the scene. A uniformed Roman Centurion, a squad of uniformed Roman marines, and a handcuffed man in a cloak. He quickly left the stall, calling a young boy and a slave out with him.

Vulso threw the thin man against the wall and closed the shutters, sealing off the shop from watchers on the street. The only light was provided by the eerie red glow of the blacksmith's furnace. The prisoner looked terrified.

"Where'd you get that book?" asked Vulso again.

The thin man spat at him.

Vulso smashed him in the face, knocking out three teeth. Blood spurted from the man's nose and mouth. Vulso then kicked him in the groin, and when he went down, booted him hard in the stomach. The Centurion let him writhe and groan and then picked him up and chopped him on the collar bone. He screamed in agony and went down again. Vulso picked him up and sat him on a chair and without saying a word picked up a pair of metal tongs. The Centurion put on a blacksmith's glove and held the tongs over the hot coals of the furnace, while his captive gasped in pain and watched in horror.

"No, don't," he said weakly. "I told you I don't know anything."

Vulso ignored him, took the tongs from the fire and approached him. The tongs were glowing red.

"No, please," croaked the thin man. Vulso ripped open his cloak and tunic with his free hand and let the heat of the tongs radiate into the man's chest and then into his face.

"No," he screamed. "Don't."

Vulso brought the burning hot metal closer.

He began to scream in terror. "Isarion," he yelled. "I got it from Isarion the antiques dealer."

The man began to cry as Vulso backed off and doused the tongs in a vat of water. The Centurion opened the shutters and let in the light.

XXIII

THE TRIAL OF SECUNDUS BEGINS

The trial of Secundus for judicial murder under the *Lex Cornelia* started precisely at the 3rd morning hour. Proculus called the court to order and the judge and his assessor filed in behind two lictors, each carrying a bundle of rods enclosing an axe, the symbol of magisterial power. Severus took his seat on the Tribunal and surveyed the scene.

Secundus, draped in a defendant's black toga to show tragedy and evoke sympathy, occupied the bench on one side of the front row with his lawyer, while the lawyer's entourage of clerks and assistants, all dressed in white, sat to the side and behind them. On the other side of the front row sat the prosecution witnesses, including several of the women from the House of Selene.

The benches for spectators were packed with eminent looking men in togas over broad and narrow striped Senatorial and Equestrian tunics. Secundus had his friends out in force. And in the midst of them was the Prefect himself. It was a strong show of support for Secundus.

Behind the benches, in the semi-circular standing room area at the back of the courtroom was a crowd of people in ordinary tunics. Severus judged from the winks, smiles and whispering going on among them that they were the private claque of Secundus' lawyer, hired to attend the trial and cheer for points in Secundus' favor, while razzing the opposition.

Judge Severus braced himself. He had plenty of experience with Roman courtroom claques. He could handle them, but the chore was always unpleasant. And he would be under the scrutiny of powerful government officials whose support of the defendant was evident.

Severus signaled to Proculus to begin reading the charges. A slightly sinister murmur emanated from the back of the courtroom. Severus asked the defendant's lawyer if he wished to make any statements before taking evidence.

The lawyer, a large boisterous looking man, with a red face and bulbous nose, took an orator's stance in front of the tribunal and introduced himself as Septimus Eggius.

"Judge," announced Eggius, "I request an adjournment."

"On what grounds?" responded Severus.

"We are waiting for the arrival of a witness, without whom we cannot possibly defend ourselves."

"And who is this witness?"

"His name is Isarion, judge. He is presently on the island of Rhodes, but last week I sent a messenger requesting him to return to Alexandria as quickly as possible. He should be on his way, but he has not yet arrived."

"Do you have other witnesses or evidence to present besides Isarion?"

"Well, yes, judge, we do, but Isarion is a most critical witness and I..."

Severus interrupted him. "We can then proceed with the trial as far as possible and later adjourn for a reasonable time to await Isarion if you feel then that his testimony is still necessary. Therefore, I deny the motion for an adjournment."

There was a commotion among the audience, both the eminent observers on the benches and the not so eminent ones standing in the back. Severus waited a few moments in silence for the disturbance to subside. It didn't.

He called for order and cautioned the spectators against outbursts in a manner both polite and threatening.

"I will open the trial by putting certain documents in evidence," announced the judge, beginning the case against Secundus. Proculus read from the list the judge had given him, which included the file of the case so far, including Ganymede's confession. He then began calling as witnesses the courtesans from the House of Selene. Aurora, the red-haired woman who had shared the Prefect's couch, was first and reviewed the events from the time the *hetairai* arrived to the death of Titus Pudens. Under careful guidance from questioning by the judge, she was led to emphasize the riotous behavior of the defendant almost as much as to establish that Ganymede never had an opportunity to be near the Prefect's couch. Her testimony was supported by Andromache, the woman who had been paired with the missing Homeric scholar Philogenes. She was the one who remembered Ganymede behind her couch, and not near the Prefect's. There was also testimony from the other courtesans at the party. Although each courtesan admitted she sometimes didn't see what was going on, in total they seemed to nullify the possibility that Ganymede could have poisoned the Prefect's drinking cup.

Affidavits were read into the record from the Prefect, saying he was too drunk to remember anything, and from the Isis priest Petamon to the same effect.

Then the judge produced a surprise witness: one of the young slave-girls of the Prefect who had served his couch during the orgy. She had been interviewed secretly in the judge's chambers in the hour before court convened. The 12-year-old was quite charming and earned the Prefect many admiring glances from the officials in the audience. But Secundus went pale as she supported the testimony of the courtesans that Ganymede was in another part of the room and had never approached the Prefect's couch.

"I knew all along that Ganymede couldn't have tried to kill the master," she volunteered. "But no one ever asked me before you did, *kyrie*."

Severus dismissed her and then had Proculus read the statement of the torturer Rufus, blaming Secundus for ordering excessive pain. Then Severus turned to Secundus' lawyer.

"Your client, Eggius, appears on the evidence to have wrongly procured the confession and execution of an innocent man, just as the charge sheet accuses. What is your defense?"

This was Eggius' moment. He sensed the urging of the crowd behind him. He took an orator's stance, moved his arm out in a wide dramatic sweep, and spoke.

"To paraphrase the immortal Cicero," he began in stentorian voice, "it is the beginning of my defense which causes me the greatest anxiety, for, despite my years of experience and learning, I am not sure whether my ability is worthy of defending a client so eminent as" -- he pointed to Secundus -- "a trusted member of the staff of the Prefect of Egypt. A Prefect, moreover" -- here he turned and gestured toward the Prefect in the audience -- "whose long years of service have made him an excellent judge of men as well of affairs."

A burst of applause and cheers from the claque greeted the compliment to the Prefect. Calvus nodded and smiled in acknowledgment.

"Not only that," continued Eggius, "my client is not only of the Prefect's governmental family, as it were, but also a member of his own family -- his stepson."

The attribution drew more applause.

Severus called the court to order sharply. The lictors snapped their bundles of rods and axes to attention. The crowd settled down.

Eggius paced the floor in front of the Tribunal, his head down. When there was sufficient silence, he stopped suddenly, and looked right at the judge. He pointed to his client. "And I have proof, judge, proof of the most persuasive kind, that Secundus is innocent."

The crowd clapped loudly.

"What is my proof?" asked Eggius rhetorically. "It is that Secundus can be guilty only if Ganymede is innocent. But I have new proof that Ganymede is guilty. Convincing, positive proof." He stopped dramatically. The crowd hung on his words. Severus bent forward in his chair with an interested look.

Eggius reached into the folds of his toga and pulled out a scroll. He held it above his head.

"This document! This document proves that Ganymede is guilty and that, therefore, Secundus is innocent!"

The crowd cheered. Eggius waved the scroll above his head. With a motion of his hands, the lawyer silenced his claque and turned to the judge.

"I call to the Tribunal the witnesses Nefertari and Herakleia, slaves of the scholar Philogenes."

Severus, Flaccus and Proculus exchanged looks. The old woman and the young girl who Severus had interviewed some time before at Philogenes' apartment came up to the Tribunal. Eggius asked them to identify the seal on the document the lawyer held. They both said it was the personal seal of their master, the Homeric scholar Philogenes.

"He always had it with him," said the old woman. "It had an engraving he liked." She pointed to the seal impression. "A scene from Homer."

"You may continue, Eggius," said Severus mildly.

Eggius dismissed the witnesses and addressed the judge and the courtroom.

"This document, sealed with the seal of the famous Homeric scholar Philogenes, who was himself at the Prefect's party, states positively that he, Philogenes, saw with his own eyes the slave Ganymede pour wine into the Prefect's dolphin cup."

The claque burst into uncontrolled cheers. Eggius waved the scroll once again, as if cheering on the claque with it. Eggius then motioned them to be silent and turned grandly to the judge.

"I offer it in evidence."

The crowd cheered again. Secundus was beaming from ear to ear.

So was Vulso. So was Severus.

A clerk brought the scroll from Eggius to the judge. Severus took it, inspected the seal, and broke it. Then

he turned to Proculus and nodded. Proculus in turn nodded to a clerk standing by the door and the clerk left the
courtroom. Severus watched him go and then opened
the scroll, relaxed in his chair and slowly read it. Eggius
kept the crowd respectfully silent during the judge's
reading. Severus made a show of finishing, let the document furl up, and asked a question.

"I understand, Eggius, that this Homeric scholar
Philogenes has disappeared?"

"That's true, judge," answered Eggius quickly. "But as
you can see from the date, he executed the document before the date of his disappearance. And his affidavit is good
evidence, judge, since we can't locate the witness himself."

"Was this document sealed before witnesses?" asked
the judge.

"Yes, as a matter of fact," answered Eggius. "It was
made in the presence of my client, Secundus, in his office
in the Hadrianum. Philogenes executed it as evidence
in the case against Ganymede, in the normal course of
Secundus' investigation. The investigation," he sneered,
"that is alleged to have been faulty and incomplete."

"Then why wasn't it in the file that Secundus showed
me when I first arrived?" asked Severus skeptically.

"It had been misplaced in another file," answered
Eggius in a tone suggesting honest mistake. "A clerical
error, judge."

"I see," said Severus cynically. "In other words,
Secundus knew of this document's existence all along
but chose not to bring it to my attention before now. Not
when I first talked to him or when I first put it to him that
Ganymede was innocent."

The lawyer cleared his throat. He had anticipated the
question and had an answer for it.

"My client, judge, was so shocked by this baseless accusation, that he lost his composure in your presence. When he told me about this document, it was felt it was better to present it in open court in order to squelch these charges once and for all. After all, judge, what is on the other side. Only the testimony by some women that they didn't see what they may not have been looking at. But Philogenes saw, and he saw Ganymede do it."

The lawyer looked even more smug than Secundus. A few notables in the audience began audibly congratulating the defendant.

"Secundus to the Tribunal!" snapped Judge Severus. The defendant looked at his lawyer uncertainly. Eggius also looked uncertain but indicated that he should stand before the Tribunal. Secundus did so.

Severus glared at the figure in the black toga. The judge was fully prepared for what was going to happen in the courtroom. He saw two clerks enter the court, one with a sealed box, the other with a sheaf of affidavits, and station themselves against the wall.

Severus shot his questions at Secundus. "Were you present when Philogenes sealed this document?"

"I was."

"Did it occur in your office in the Hadrianum?"

"It did."

"Was the date the" -- Severus checked the document -- "third day before the Kalends of June?"

"Yes."

"Do you swear an oath that you witnessed it at that time and place?"

"I do."

"Who found this affidavit of Philogenes?"

"I did."

"When?"

"When I went back to my office after I was granted bail."

"Where did you find it?"

"In the file of another case. The one right next to Ganymede's in my file box."

"You are to return to your seat, Secundus. Caius Vulso to the Tribunal."

The big Centurion pushed his way through the crowd and stood before Judge Severus. He described concisely how a few days ago he had entered the apartment Secundus had shared with Cupid while both were out and how he had searched it. He then told what he found.

"It was on the table right next to Secundus' travel bag. It was the draft of an affidavit being forged. An affidavit allegedly from the scholar Philogenes, claiming he saw Ganymede pour wine into the Prefect's cup. At the time I saw it, it was undated and unfinished and covered with red editing marks."

"Did you make an exact copy of this document and have it placed under seal of a Roman court that very day?"

"I did."

The clerk holding the box was called forward. The affidavits of the two court clerks who had witnessed Vulso's copy being placed into the box were read into evidence. The seal on the box was opened and the copy of the incompletely forged Philogenes affidavit was taken out.

The judge had both documents brought to him and held open in front of him for comparison. "It is obvious," said the judge studying both, "that the writing the Centurion found a few days ago was an incomplete draft of the complete document that the defendant alleges was presented to him weeks before. To be complete before it was incomplete presents almost a proof by contradiction in the geometry of Euclid, a *reductio ad absurdum*, a logical impossibility. Therefore, the defendant's so-called evidence must be false."

By that time pandemonium was reigning in the courtroom. Secundus had turned grey; Eggius green. The Prefect's mouth hung open. All the dignitaries looked at the walls and floors or cast hostile glances toward Secundus.

"Prepare the charge sheets," ordered Judge Severus to his clerk. "Secundus to stand trial for the additional crimes of forgery and perjury."

He addressed Eggius. "Do you still wish to adjourn until Isarion arrives?" asked Severus maliciously, "or do you want to proceed to a verdict on the judicial murder charge now?"

"I wish an adjournment," said the lawyer, recovering rapidly. "Isarion's testimony is now vital, whatever the facts of that unfortunate document, from which, judge, I completely disassociate myself. I did not know it was a forgery when I offered it. I hope you will believe that I was fooled in this matter."

Severus nodded politely at him. "We will adjourn this trial for a few days until we find out whether Isarion is able to join us.

"Until then, of course, bail will be revoked on Secundus. He will be placed in the Hadrianum's detention cells until the next session of the court."

Severus stood up from the Tribunal.

"Court is adjourned!" declared Proculus.

XXIV

THE PREFECT INTERVENES

The next morning Severus received a message from the Prefect that he was to come to the Prefect's office at the 2nd hour of the morning. It was important, though the message didn't say why.

Severus arrived on time and was shown in to see the Prefect. Calvus was pacing back and forth in front of the portraits of the Emperors. There was no food or drink on the table between the couches and the Prefect neither exchanged greeting kisses with the judge nor invited him to recline. His whole manner seemed unfriendly, his face was hardened and his voice hostile.

"I've been thinking over the matter of your trial of my stepson," he began directly, "and I'm disturbed by your ever widening attempt to pillory him. Now you are not only after Secundus for the Ganymede situation but also for manufacturing false evidence. In addition you are investigating stolen books and false antiques. These are not part of your mission, Severus, so I'm beginning to think that you have a personal grudge against Secundus, that you are obsessed with him, persecuting him."

"I am following where the evidence leads, Prefect, trying to find who has a motive to poison you. In this investigation, it is coming to light that Secundus may be involved in, even directing a ring that is stealing books from the Great Library and manufacturing and distributing phony antiques, along with your friend Isarion. Whether or not this bears on the attempt to kill you, I don't know yet."

"Severus, all this is really none of your business. Secundus is not part of your mission. That being the case, as Prefect of Egypt, I have decided to refer the Secundus case directly to the Emperor in Rome. That is my right as Prefect and it is Secundus' right as a Roman citizen to appeal to the Emperor. He is therefore now immune from your further harassment. Your trial of Secundus is as of this moment at an end. I am releasing him from bail and putting him under my own recognizance."

"I have to disagree with you," countered Severus. "Secundus' false execution of the slave Ganymede is a case of judicial murder under Roman law. Since I am a special judge of Rome, the Emperor's *iudex selectus*, it certainly is my business to bring him to trial.

"However, I have to acknowledge Secundus' right as a Roman citizen to appeal for a trial before the Emperor and your right as Prefect to refer the case to Rome."

"And there is something else," continued Calvus in his same hard tone of voice. "I understand that your operatives have been snooping around at the Imperial Post, asking questions about Pudens."

"That is correct, Prefect. You claim no one at the orgy had a motive to kill you. If that's true, though I'm not convinced of it, it's then possible that the person who died is the person for whom the poison was meant.

Logic dictates that I pursue that possibility and therefore I am investigating whether anyone had a motive to kill Pudens."

Calvus smiled. He had the answer he wanted. "In that case, Severus, I have now concluded that Pudens was in fact the person for whom the poison was intended, not me. Since you were assigned to find who tried to kill me, and since the answer now is no one, your assignment from the Emperor is at an end."

"In that case, Prefect," replied Severus with an edge to his voice, "since you conclude that Pudens was the intended victim, then you must conclude that Ganymede's confession saying he tried to kill *you* is false and therefore Secundus is guilty of ...

Calvus cut him off. "Severus, I no longer wish to continue this discussion. You have my decision. I am standing by my stepson. Your trial of Secundus is at an end. Your mission in Alexandria is at an end. You may return to Rome or tour Egypt, whatever you like. Maybe in about a year, when the case of Secundus reaches the Emperor, if it does, you might look in on his trial, if there ever is one."

Calvus glared at Severus with a challenging stare, almost in the manner of one gladiator facing off against another.

Severus glared back at Calvus just as challengingly, angry at his interference with justice. He then turned and walked out.

Whatever his outward appearance, inwardly Severus was smiling, content. Not only would he now be free to spend a few weeks touring the sites of Egypt -- the pyramids, the Sphinx, -- but the case against Secundus would be moved to Rome. His ground, more than the Prefect's.

After a few steps in the marbled hall, he slowed down and stopped. An ironic, but uncomfortable, thought had occurred to him. He felt almost a sense of betraying Marcus Aurelius. The Emperor had sent him to Egypt to find out who had tried to kill the Prefect and to protect him from further harm. But he had not discovered who poisoned the Prefect's cup and now he could no longer protect Calvus because, as a result of his own actions, he was being thrown out of the province. His mission, to put it bluntly, was a total failure.

MARCUS FLAVIUS SEVERUS: TO HIMSELF

Everything is in abeyance, unresolved. I don't know who put poison in the Prefect's cup. I don't even know whether the poison was intended for Calvus or for the victim Pudens. Moreover, Philogenes, the librarian and Homeric scholar, has not been found. Isarion is possibly a forger of antiquities and complicit in stealing books from the Great Library, but he is in Rhodes. Serpentinus, the Prefect's aide, is unavailable. Claudius Celer, the Imperial Post aide of the victim Pudens, has either been sent away or fled. And the case of judicial murder against Secundus has been referred to the Emperor in Rome, while the Prefect has virtually ordered me out of the province, declaring my mission at an end.

But I was still in Egypt and I was not going to miss seeing to the pyramids and the other tourist wonders of the country. So with Artemisia and my whole staff we went up-country for a few weeks. The Prefect even provided us with a guide and an escort. I accepted, even though I knew the escort was also there to make sure I didn't do any more investigating. But I wasn't that docile. I made sure before I left to gather affidavits from the witnesses I had interviewed. I got written statements from all the *hetairai* and the young slave girls about Ganymede's non-presence at the Prefect's couch; I got a statement from the *quaestionarius'* telling his story of how Secundus had asked Ganymede leading and suggestive questions and ordered excessive pain. If there was going to be a trial before the Emperor, I wanted to have the case against Secundus fully documented.

Meanwhile, the pyramids. They were astonishing. Covered in smooth, gleaming white limestone they appeared almost unearthly, to descend to Earth from the sky like rays of light. This is how they were intended to look. We are told by the Egyptian priests, who keep the records, that the pyramids are more than 2,500 years old. One can therefore appreciate why past ages are often seen as golden ages and why our age is often compared to lesser debased metal.

Once the famous Curator of Waters for the City of Rome, Julius Frontinus, called the pyramids useless when compared to the great aqueducts of Rome, which send millions of gallons of water into the City everyday. The pyramids useless? Not to my mind. Certainly not as practical as the aqueducts of Rome, but beauty and wonder are not useless and the pyramids are beautiful and wondrous.

In the same vein, Pliny said he preferred Rome's great sewer, the Cloaca Maxima, to the Sphinx because of the sewer's utility. But I am not a sewer enthusiast and now having seen the Sphinx, I disagree with Pliny. I prefer the Sphinx.

So maybe Vulso is right when he often questions how 'Roman' I am. But to my mind his interpretation of 'Roman' is too narrow. I'm sure, for instance, that

Marcus Aurelius, if he had the opportunity to see the pyramids and the Sphinx, as the Emperor Hadrian did, would also admire them.

In any case, this is a cosmopolitan age and there is no reason to make that kind of choice. I also admire our aqueducts and appreciate the utility of the great sewer. These are wonders in their own right.

To complete our tour we traveled further up-country to Thebes to see the Colossi of Memnon and hear the "singing" statue. One of the Colossi actually made a sound as the Sun rose at the 1st hour in the morning. But the sound it made, if it was the statue that made it and not the heating of the Sun or the whistling of the wind or a trick of the Egyptian priests, was not that impressive, though it was strange. We also saw the ancient rock-cut tombs of the pharaohs, all robbed long ago, though some mummies and mummy parts were still gruesomely left around. The tombs were impressively constructed and decorated and worth seeing. But we all agreed that a graffito left by an earlier traveler just about summed it up: "I, Philaestrios the Alexandrian, who came to Thebes and saw these tombs of astounding horror, have had a delightful day."

So after an interesting and exciting tour of the wonders of Egypt and its famous tourist sites, we returned to Alexandria, boarded the warship *Argo* and returned home to Rome.

SCROLL II

SEVERUS IN ROME

MARCUS FLAVIUS SEVERUS: TO HIMSELF

Home!

The trip back from Alexandria to Rome took twice as long as the two-week trip out. The prevailing winds blowing from west to east made sailing west more difficult and the weather, as summer was coming to an end, was worse. Still we made it.

And there is nothing like a homecoming. We landed in Ostia, sent a message ahead that we had landed and took a coach from there to our home on the Caelian Hill in Rome. Everyone was there. Family first. The children were overjoyed to see us, as much as we were overjoyed to see them.

Aulus, Flavia and Quintus regaled us with hugs and kisses and voluble non-stop talking. Our dog Argos couldn't stop barking in joy and running around in circles and jumping on both me and Artemisia. Even Phaon, our usually taciturn cat, kept brushing his side against our legs. He was also happy to have us back in his home.

The slaves made us a wonderful meal and we distributed our presents to the children and to the slaves, who are also a treasured part of our *familia*. Everyone got a beautiful inlaid Egyptian box and a blue faiance scarab with "life, prosperity, health" hieroglyphs. Artemisia had in the end bought about 30 of each, not only for each member of the *familia* but also for friends.

We caught up on news and told stories of our trip and what we had seen. The trip 500 feet up to the top of the Lighthouse brought the most exclamations of "*babae*" and "*papae*" – wonderful.

Then we spent a few days together, visiting friends, having friends visit us, and just getting back to our normal life.

Then it was time to report to the Emperor.

XXV

SEVERUS REPORTS TO THE EMPEROR

"You know, Severus," confided Marcus Aurelius, as they sat at a table in the peristyle of the Domus Flavia, Aurelius' private residence on the Palatine, "early every morning I say to myself, today I shall meet with people who are interfering, ungrateful, hubristic, deceitful, envious and selfish."

"Not all in one day, I hope," replied Severus.

Aurelius laughed. "No, but probably one of each of them during the course of one week. There are good men too, of course, and I look forward to meeting those, as I did to this meeting with you."

"Thank you, *domine*."

"I actually still remember playing *trigon* with you, and one game in particular where you bluffed me to look one way and threw the ball into my face, giving me a bloody nose. I was very angry at the time, but my mother said I should respect the boy who treated me like any other playmate and not like some special person who should be deferred to. I always remembered that, and I

feel you will still treat me that way now – like a fellow
citizen – the way I want to be treated, despite calling me
domine."

"I will, *domine*. I can act in no other way."

"Good. What I prize personally is the exercise of the
intellect and fellowship with kindred spirits. And I feel
you and I are similar in that way. So I know I can rely
on your concern for justice and the unembellished truth.
I got that sense from your letters and reports about what
happened in Alexandria and from my own instinct about
people."

It was a week after Severus' return to Rome. A report to the Emperor was his official priority and he had
submitted one, complete with the affidavits of witnesses
in Alexandria and the transcript of the court proceedings,
transcribed by his court clerk. Aurelius was anxious to
discuss it. On the table between them were elegant color-
less, translucent glasses containing mulsum, white wine
with honey. Aurelius took a sip. "Like Augustus I savor
mulsum. 'Oil for the outside', he said, 'but mulsum for
the inside'." Severus also sipped his drink. A snack of
chickpeas in small bowls was also on the table as was
an elegant box containing *theriac* – pills of *tranquilli-
tas*. The opium based pills were a popular 'remedy' for
overworked and stressed out people, as well as for those
who just enjoyed the effect of the drug. The Emperor,
on the advice of his physician Galen, was a regular user,
not only to counter the stresses of his office, but also to
help fight his chronic chest and stomach pains. Severus,
however, stayed away from the pills.

Aurelius returned to the subject of the meeting. "I
was distressed, as were you, by the execution of an innocent person, the slave Ganymede, and also by the charge

of judicial murder lodged against the Prefect's stepson. I understand you had no choice as a Roman judge but to bring him to trial. Since the Prefect of Egypt has referred the case to me --an *appellatio* to the Emperor -- I have little choice but to entertain it. I have therefore called Calvus to Rome for consultations and his stepson here for trial.

"But first, tell me what you think happened. I am still not quite clear on that. Was the Prefect the intended victim? Or was it the person who actually died, Pudens? And who do you think is the poisoner?"

"I don't know the answer to those questions, *domine*. I didn't have the opportunity to complete the investigation. For instance, I have not been able to question three participants in the orgy – the missing librarian Philogenes, the shady antique dealer Isarion or the the Prefect's aide, Serpentinus. So I can't really assess their motives. Also I would like to question Pudens' assistant, Claudius Celer. He was either transferred out of Egypt back to Rome or fled in fear. In the end, the Prefect effectively cut off my investigation and ordered me out of Egypt.

"As far as Claudius Celer is concerned, if he is in Rome, I can continue my investigation here. But he hasn't shown up at the Imperial Post headquarters in the City. I've checked."

Aurelius thought a bit. "I can see it would be useful to find Celer. So I will assign the Praetorian Guard to help you. They can comb the City and find him. I want you to direct their efforts."

"That's a good idea and I will direct them."

"Good," answered Aurelius, swallowing down a tranquility pill with a drink of mulsum. "Now I have to keep an independent mind since the trial of Secundus is coming to my court, so let's talk about something else -- our childhood, for instance."

Severus smiled as memories came back. "Another thing I remember besides playing ball with you was when you told the other chicks that you slept on the floor. I even tried it once myself, but didn't like it."

Aurelius smiled. "I remember that too. When as a child I first studied philosophy, I thought I should adopt the habits of a philosopher, so I wore a rough cloak and slept on the floor. My mother didn't like it at all and though I was reluctant she finally persuaded me to sleep on a small palette covered with hides. I was a serious child, you see. And that seriousness was one of the reasons the Emperor Hadrian, who was a family friend and used to visit us even after my father died, picked me out to be educated and trained to become the Emperor. Involuntarily, I should add."

"You didn't want to become Emperor?"

"I was appalled. And I've always carried something of a grudge against Hadrian because of it. I became one of his projects to improve the Empire. He took hold of my life and turned it to what he wanted. You see, Severus, I really wanted to be a writer of history books." Aurelius smiled, almost ruefully. "I still take notes from my readings for some future day, which probably will never come, when I can write those books."

"But you can be a great Emperor. A philosopher on the throne. Just as Plato envisioned." Severus quoted the famous words of Plato. "States flourish if philosophers rule or if rulers are philosophers."

"I sometimes think that there are few better positions than Emperor to put philosophy into practical use," replied Aurelius, "as long as I take care not to be dyed in the purple. However other times I'm not so sure. Being Emperor by its very nature can be incompatible with leading a philosophic life. Ruling sometimes must betray philosophy."

He looked directly at Severus, with an expression now more knowing and realistic than rueful.

"So don't expect Plato's Republic."

XXVI

THE SEARCH FOR
CLAUDIUS CELER

"The Praetorian Guard?" exclaimed Vulso, when the next day in chambers Severus told him about his conference with the Emperor. "We're supposed to work with those arrogant *effeminati*?"

His words and tone expressed both the resentment of members of the Urban Cohort who were looked down on by the Praetorian Guard as socially beneath them and the scorn of a veteran of the legions who looked down on the Praetorian Guard as militarily incompetent.

"There won't be a problem," said Severus, who understood the long standing rivalries and frictions. "The Emperor has personally instructed the Praetorian Prefect that there's to be harmonious cooperation in this matter."

Vulso snorted. "There have been times, you may recall, judge, when it was the Praetorian Guard that instructed the Emperors."

"That was more than 60 years ago. Nowadays, the Guard is loyal and obedient. Both Praetorian Prefects are career officials devoted to the regime and to the Emperor. There won't be any problems."

"I hope you're right," replied Vulso doubtfully because Severus' brush off was somewhat tendentious. They both knew, as did everyone else, that just two years before, upon their accession, Marcus Aurelius and Lucius Verus, like all other Emperors before them since the time of Claudius, first met with the Senate and then went directly to the camp of the Praetorian Guard. There they addressed the troops and promised a special donative of 20,000 sesterces per man, almost 10-years pay. Only then did the new Emperors receive the support and acclamation of the Guard. So while the Praetorians might now be loyal and obedient, as Severus phrased it, they first had to be generously paid off for their compliance.

A little while later a Tribune of the Praetorian Guard showed up at the judge's chambers in the rooms behind the colonnades inside the Forum of Augustus. He parked a detachment of guardsmen in the forum itself. On duty at the palace, guardsmen were required to wear civilian togas, with their swords concealed underneath, in conformity with the traditional policy and practice of the Emperors to display Republican forms of government instead of imperial realities. No one was more congenially attached to this policy than Marcus Aurelius. But here, away from the palace, the Tribune and guardsmen were in full dress uniforms – red tunic, square red cloak, wearing the new style helmets, with bars of reinforcement strips replacing the crests, and shields displaying the insignia of the Praetorian Guard – a scorpion. It was the horoscope sign of the Emperor Tiberius, one of the founders of the Guard.

But whether in civilian or military dress, all the guardsmen were paid three times the salary of a legionary and had only 3/5 the length of service. Just as agreeably, their service was spent mostly in cosmopolitan Rome and not in camps on wild and dangerous frontiers, though in the current crisis of war with Persia, part of the Guard was actually at the front with one of the Prefects and the co-emperor Lucius Verus.

The Tribune introduced himself as Publius Cornelius Naso, with his voice emphasizing 'Cornelius', an old distinguished Roman family name. Arrogance was unabashedly on display.

Severus ignored it. "We have a job to do, as you know. We must find a certain Claudius Celer, an official of the Imperial Post. He left his position in Alexandria, either expelled or fled in fear, supposedly to come back to Rome. But he has not turned up at the Imperial Post offices here.

"The first step, therefore, was to ask people who know him at the Imperial Post where he lives and where he might be. We have done that already and found that he lived with his family in an apartment in the Subura. But he and his family are not there and neighbors don't know where they are. Celer told the neighbors he was moving, but did not say where."

Cornelius was doubtful. "Counting slaves and foreigners and visitors, there are probably around two million people in the City at any time. How are we supposed to find one person?"

"We search. Talk again with his colleagues at the Imperial Post, with their neighbors in the Subura and probe more deeply. Start today and report to me every few days or so. I want to know everything about Celer, who his friends were, what his interests are, what he might be doing now. If he's not working at the Imperial Post, what could he be doing to earn a living? And include information about his wife and the children as well. Are they in school? Where?"

Cornelius saluted and left.

Two days later Cornelius returned in a bad mood with a report of no progress. "We found out nothing. No one will talk to us."

"In that case," suggested Severus, "try bribery."

"Bribery? How much should we pay?"

"20,000 sesterces per person might work," replied Severus with a straight face.

"20,000 sesterces? But that's the same amount that each guardsman was paid when the new Emperors acceded to.... Oh, I see, you're joking, aren't you?"

Severus didn't answer. Cornelius first looked like he was going to be indignant, but then broke out in a huge laugh. "Oh yes, judge, 20,000 sesterces per person. That's very good. I must tell it to everyone. 20,000 sesterces." He chortled, saluted and left in a good mood.

XXVII

ARTEMISIA TAKES SEVERUS TO THE SAEPTA JULIA MARKET

Two days later, a warm, sunny beautiful afternoon, while the search for Claudius Celer was still in progress, Artemisia came by Severus' courthouse in the Forum of Augustus. She asked him to walk with her up the Via Lata – 'Broadway' – to the Saepta Julia marketplace.

"What for?" he asked. "We usually shop at Trajan's Market right next door. Why do we have to go to the Saepta? It's up by the Pantheon."

"There's something I want to show you there. Besides on a beautiful afternoon like today it will nice just to walk there."

Severus saw something in his wife's demeanor. She showed a sort of curious self-satisfied smile, as if to say, in the common expression, that she 'had Jupiter by the balls.'

"And by the way," she added, "put on a plain toga, not your judicial toga."

He just gave her a quizzical look. Now he was intrigued.

They walked up the Via Lata, Severus in a plain white toga, Artemisia in a pale blue stola, with an orange belt. Broadway was crowded with afternoon activity, a motley street crowd of strollers, shoppers, bustling workers, idlers and street loungers, messengers darting in and out of the crowd, school children returning home, the whole gamut of every day life, from elegance to riff-raff, from senators to slaves. There were plenty of litters, but they caused a lot of the traffic jams, making walking a more desirable and certainly faster way of moving, even if not so ostentatious. Still pedestrian traffic was thick enough to cause rubbing of elbows and rushing people bumping into each other, as crowds thickened and thinned like the action of waves. The din was palpable. And the shops lining the street and in the porticoes were all busy as were the entrepreneurs set up on the sidewalks -- barbers and doctors, food vendors hawking their cakes and sausages and snacks and drinks, street musicians, rhetoricians and haranguing hucksters, magicians, fortune-tellers, beggars and lunatics.

Severus and Artemisia stopped at a street-side taverna with a counter facing the sidewalk. They had a snack of salt and pepper chickpeas and cups of mulsum, honeyed white wine, while standing on the street by the counter, observing people. Then they continued along still enjoying the vibrancy of street life, though not enjoying other people brushing too closely by them in their hurried and oblivious rush to get wherever they were going. Still they reached the Saepta Julia in good time.

The Saepta – the 'enclosure' – was a quadroportico, a four-sided columned building enclosing a large rectangle almost 1,000 feet long and 300 feet wide. In the time of the Republic it had been a meeting place for voting assemblies and ballot booths. When the Empire came, Augustus substituted gladiatorial shows for democratic elections, and later it became what it was now – a large marketplace with especially expensive and elegant shops inside, along with art works decorating the walkways and the interior square and buildings. The inside shops were high-class and very costly. Citrus wood tables with ivory legs, tortoise shell decorated divans, Corinthian bronzes, crystal vases, fluorspar bowls, antique chalices, exquisite jewelry, emeralds set in gold, large pearls, jasper, sardonyx, statuary by famous artists and every other type of item that could attract wealthy buyers ready to spend money. Merchandise that could fetch a high price, whether it was worth it or not, was the fare inside the Saepta Julia.

"So what have we come to buy?" asked Severus suspiciously, as they entered through the portico facing the Via Lata and headed toward the more expensive inner shops.

"We're not here to buy, so much as to look. And at one shop in particular. An antiques store, and it's just down this lane. I found it this morning when I came with my friend Valeria. She wanted to buy a citrus wood table, but the store next door drew my attention. There it is," she pointed.

It was an antiques store she pointed at. In front were displayed Egyptian style items -- statues, boxes, bowls.

Severus saw the sign outside. "The Golden Ibis," he read out loud. "Antiques from Egypt."

The name jogged his memory.

"You weren't in the 'The Golden Ibis' when we were in Alexandria," Artemisia said, "but I was. It was one of the two antique shops I visited." Severus raised his eyebrows. "It was the one owned by Isarion," she said.

"Isarion? You don't mean the Isarion who was at the Prefect's orgy. The one who left for Rhodes before we could talk to him. The one we never found?"

"That's exactly who I mean. And what's more, I talked to him yesterday inside that shop. I told him I had been in a shop in Alexandria with the same name. He acknowledged that The Golden Ibis in Alexandria was also his shop, as was a 'Golden Ibis' in Rhodes. He's the Isarion you've been looking for. And he may even be there right now." Her smile told it all. Severus was stunned and pleased at the same time.

But Isarion was not inside, though an obsequious clerk in an Egyptian headdress recognized Artemisia from earlier in the day and showed her and her husband the expensive gold and faience encrusted mosaic box she had showed interest in that morning.

"We must discuss price with the owner," said Artemisia.

"He will be here tomorrow, *domina*," the clerk replied. "Whatever time is convenient for you."

"The 3rd hour of the morning," interjected Severus. "We can be here then."

"Then I will make sure he will be here at that time."

They left the shop. "We'll come back tomorrow morning," he told Artemisia. "With Vulso and a squad of the Urban Cohort."

Now Severus also had a smile that said he had Jupiter by the balls. Or at least Isarion.

XXVIII

ISARION IS QUESTIONED AND CLAUDIUS CELER IS FOUND

"How is Isarion?" asked Severus at the 5th hour the next morning.

"Shaking like a leaf," answered Vulso, "and I didn't even threaten him --- much."

"Good. Bring him up from the basement to my chambers. I'll talk to him here."

Isarion was brought up to Severus' chambers in the Forum of Augustus by Vulso and dumped into a chair. He was a thin, wiry man, with pinched cheeks and very little hair. He cringed from Severus and Vulso with haunted eyes. He still wore the elegant linen tunic he had on when arrested, though it was by now somewhat rumpled.

Severus pulled up a chair and placed it directly in front of Isarion. Vulso sat on a stool on Severus' left, with an opaque smile that Isarion probably read as malevolent.

"Now," began Severus, "I know you are involved with books stolen from the Library of Alexandria, particularly the *Wisdom of Ben Sira* which we recovered from one of your henchmen."

Isarion began to protest.

Severus held up a hand to silence him. "Don't bother to deny it. Because I also know about the fake antiques you are selling in your store in Alexandria and probably selling here in Rome as well. Do you know what that means for a foreigner in Rome? It could be the lions or the panthers or the bears. Vulso, have we had an expert check every item in 'The Golden Ibis' here in Rome?"

"Not yet."

"Well, Isarion, we may hold off on that or we may not, depending on how cooperative you are. So first I want to know how you got that library book?"

Isarion was turning green. He opened his mouth to say something but then closed it.

"I'm waiting," said Severus mildly.

"I..., I..." was all Isarion could manage.

"I'm still waiting, but I'm not going to wait much longer." His voice became harsher. Vulso's smile turned from arguably to unarguably malevolent.

Isarion began shaking again. But he managed an answer. "I got it from Philogenes, the librarian."

"And how did that happen?"

"I paid him for it. He took it from the Library."

"The other books as well?"

"Yes."

"And where is Philogenes now?"

"He's dead."

"Who killed him?"

"I don't know."

"Who killed him?"

"I'm not sure."

"Who killed him?"

"Serpentinus."

"You mean the Prefect's aide? One of the guests at the orgy?"

"Yes."

"How do you know that?"

"Secundus told me. The Prefect's stepson. He was directing the thefts. I had to pay him part of the profits. He told me there would be no more books because Philogenes wanted to stop. He didn't want to do it any more and he was going to confess to the Keeper of the Books. So he said he had Serpentinus silence Philogenes, forever."

"Who else was involved in this?"

"Petamon, the Isis priest. He was working with Secundus, using his temple to fence stolen books."

"Just stolen books?"

Isarion looked pale.

"Just stolen books?" repeated Severus with a greater edge to his voice.

Isarion looked paler.

"Do I have to ask everything three times?" Severus' voice was now threatening.

"Maybe he distributed fake antiques too," he admitted wanly.

"Was the Prefect involved in any of this, the stolen books, the fake antiques?"

"Calvus? I don't know. I only sold him real antiques. It was Secundus. He ran things. He told me what to do. And he had Serpentinus kill Philogenes and then he put poison in the Prefect's cup."

"Who did?"

"Secundus did it himself. To keep the Prefect from finding out what he was doing. What else could have happened? Who else could have tried to kill the Prefect?"

"What about you?"

"Me?" he practically shouted in distress. "The Prefect was my best customer. Why ever would I want him dead? It couldn't have been me. It wasn't me. Don't think that. It had to be Secundus. It must have been him."

"Are you just guessing about this? Do you have any evidence?"

"Evidence? What evidence could I have? No one told me anything. I just think it was Secundus. That's all. He ran everything. It must have been him."

Just then someone knocked on the door and court clerk Proculus came in and whispered something into Severus' ear.

Severus got up, motioned to Vulso to come along and told Proculus to keep Isarion here, with a guard in the room with him. He walked out, with Vulso behind him.

"What's going on?" asked Vulso.

"It's Claudius Celer. The Praetorians found him and have brought him here. Right now he's in the next room. So let's go talk to him."

The Praetorian Tribune Cornelius was outside the room with a big smile on his face. "It worked judge. We bribed someone. And it didn't cost that much either. Just one gold aureus, 100 sesterces. He was living only a few streets away from his old home, so we just picked him up. He gave us no trouble either. And you'll be very interested in what he has to say."

"Good work, Cornelius," replied Severus.

Severus and Vulso entered the room. Claudius Celer was seated on a chair and looked up expectantly. He was a rather large man, bald with a rounded face, thick lips and puffed out cheeks. He wore a plain brown tunic.

"I'm Marcus Flavius Severus, judge of the Court of the Urban Prefect and this is Caius Vulso, Centurion of the Urban Cohort. We've been looking all over for you."

"I'm glad you found me. I can't take this anymore."

"What can't you take? Why were you in hiding? Why did you leave Alexandria? Why didn't you show up at your job with the Imperial Post in Rome? Why did you change your address?"

"I can answer all those questions quite simply. I was scared. I left Alexandria because I was scared."

"Scared of what?"

"That he was going to kill me. Just like he killed Pudens."

"Who is he? Who killed Pudens? Why was he killed?"

"For what he found. He was an inspector of the Imperial Post in Alexandria, as you must know. And one day he told me he came across a letter to the Prefect's stepson, Secundus, from the personal aide to an army general on the Persian front, Avidius Cassius. Pudens didn't show me the letter but he told me about it. He thought the letter was suspicious. The letter quoted Avidius Cassius calling Marcus Aurelius 'a philosophizing old woman' and Lucius Verus 'a freak of extravagance'. Pudens feared there might be a plot brewing against the Emperors, Lucius Verus at the Persian front and Marcus Aurelius in Rome. But Pudens wasn't sure and didn't know what to do about it. He was cautious. Should he warn Secundus off? And that's why he was killed. Secundus did it, he must have put poison in a cup at the orgy and saw to it that Pudens drank it. That's why

I fled. Maybe he knew Pudens told me about the conspiracy. So now I'm telling you and I'm off the hook.
I should have told you before but I didn't trust any one,
not any one."

"How did Pudens happen to read this letter?" asked
Severus. "It was sealed, wasn't it. And private."

Celer shrugged and said simply, "At the Imperial
Post letters from generals in command of legions, as well
as aides to generals in command of legions, are not always private."

Severus and Vulso left the room.

"It looks like Secundus is in a lot of trouble," said
Vulso wryly. "According to Isarion he tried to poison
the Prefect to prevent him from learning about his stolen
book ring from Philogenes. According to Celer he also
poisoned Pudens to prevent him from telling the Prefect
about a plot to kill the Emperors. They both can't be
right, can they?"

"No, they can't. Someone put poison in the Prefect's
cup, either intending to kill the Prefect or to kill Pudens.
It couldn't have been intended to kill them both. We
have to figure out which one.

"But this information is important. First, it may provide a motive for Secundus to poison the Prefect. We've
been assuming that he had no motive because his interest would be in keeping Calvus alive at least until his
adoption from stepson to son. But suppose Pudens told
Calvus about the letter to Secundus from the Persian
front. And suppose there was a confrontation between
Calvus and Secundus. And suppose Calvus threatened
not just to postpone an adoption, but to disown him, to
disinherit him because of his betrayal of the Emperors.
What then?"

"If that's so," added Vulso, "if Secundus had a motive to kill Calvus, then maybe Serpentinus did too. After all, Serpentinus may have been on the Prefect's staff, but even the Prefect told us that he was doing jobs for Secundus. And now Isarion tells us Serpentinus was ordered by Secundus to kill Philogenes. So maybe Serpentinus was actually doing Secundus' bidding, not the Prefect's."

"You're right about that, Vulso. And, of course, it also provides a motive for Secundus to kill Pudens. And maybe not only for Secundus. So what we now want to find out is what the Prefect learned from Pudens and what he told Secundus. Remember Calvus told us that Pudens made a report to him before the orgy – that's why he was at the Prefect's home in the first place. Calvus told us he didn't remember what that report was about, something trivial he claimed. But now we have to wonder."

Severus then sat down and composed a letter to the Emperor. He reported in detail what Celer had told him.

The next day, while Severus was briefing his staff, Flaccus, Vulso, Straton and Proculus, about what Isarion and Celer had told him, a messenger from the palace arrived in Severus' chambers and handed him a tablet from the Emperor. Severus opened it and read it.

M. Aurelius Antoninus, Emperor, to M. Flavius Severus, greetings:

> Your report has been discussed with my *consilium*. I am informed and you should know that the Prefect of Egypt, M. Annius Calvus, has booked passage from Alexandria to Rome on the

merchant ship *Isis*. The ship should have sailed
from Alexandria two days ago and should arrive
in Ostia 14 days from today at the earliest.

Accompanying him in his entourage are his son
Secundus, his personal aide Serpentinus, his
personal Isis priest Petamon, a scholar from the
Library of Alexandria named Philogenes, a concubine named Aurora and 27 slaves.

You will be best able to consider and determine
what is proper to be done.

Then Severus read it aloud. "Philogenes?" exclaimed
several at once. Flaccus articulated the surprise first.
"Weren't you just telling us that according to Isarion
Philogenes is dead? Murdered by Serpentinus by order
of Secundus, he said."

"That's what he told us."

"But apparently he's really alive. So where has he
been all this time?" asked Vulso. "Was he hiding from
us? And why is he showing up now all of a sudden?"

"And isn't Aurora the red-haired courtesan who was
on the Prefect's couch at the orgy?" added Flaccus.

"That was her name."

"Also Secundus is referred to as the Prefect's son,
not his stepson," noticed Proculus, "so it looks like his
adoption has been legally finalized."

"It also seems that most of the guests at the orgy are
here" observed Straton, "except for Pudens who is dead.
Even Isarion is in Rome, though we have him in our
custody."

"So what's going on?" asked Vulso, "what are they up to?"

"A good question," replied Severus. He stood up and began pacing the floor, his hands behind his back, his head tilted forward. Everyone else became silent, waiting, just waiting. They had seen him go into these reveries before, thinking things out.

After a while Severus stood up straight, a smile on his face, a gleam in his eyes. "They all must be coming to Rome for Secundus' trial before the Emperor," he said. "And I think they're going to stick to their claim that Secundus is innocent of judicial murder on the grounds that the slave Ganymede tried to poison the Prefect."

"But," interjected Proculus, "we know that's untrue. We even have them on record, don't we? The Isis priest Petamon, for instance. You got him to write out a statement saying he didn't see anything. And Aurora told you and Flaccus that Ganymede was never near the Prefect's couch. We even have the false affidavit of Philogenes that Vulso found in Secundus' apartment."

"They'll retract it all," suggested Severus. "Petamon is here to say I pressured him to write that affidavit and that now he remembers Ganymede being at the Prefect's couch. Aurora is here to say she also now remembers Ganymede at the Prefect's couch. Philogenes will probably say the same thing and that the affidavit Vulso found partially complete in Secundus' rooms is really his. Serpentinus will also finger Ganymede. The Prefect may say we framed Secundus, that I have a grudge against him. What else can they be up to? They will try to put us on trial."

"Then what do we do?" asked Straton.

"We have to be ready for them and their lies. We have at least 14 days before their ship is due to arrive and a hearing date is not yet set. We will have to demolish their case and, if necessary, destroy them in court."

"How can we do that?" asked Flaccus.

"We'll think of something," replied Severus, whose smile indicated that he already had.

XXIX

SEVERUS PREPARES FOR AN APPEAL TO THE EMPEROR AND ATTENDS A LECTURE

The next days were devoted to preparations.

The first order of business was to research the specific law and procedure on *appellatio* to the Emperor's court. Severus, Flaccus and Proculus spent two days in law libraries, reading manuals and also asking practicing lawyers about it.

"All rulers, of whatever country, including our own" said Severus somewhat didactically, when they were gathered in his chambers to discuss the matter, "hold court and personally rule on petitions of their subjects. This is an essential part of ruling. Of course, not every case can come before the Emperor, there are simply too many petitioners. So permission must first be granted to entertain an *appellatio*. If it is granted, there are different procedures for different circumstances. Primarily, though, there are two – one when there has already been a decision by a court and the other when there hasn't, when the matter comes to the Emperor in the first instance.

"When there has been a trial and a decision, the facts are already a matter of record, and lawyers for both sides argue their cases in front of the Emperor and his assessors. The Emperor then decides the case. The second situation is where the facts are not yet a matter of record. Then a hearing or trial has to be held, either before the Emperor or first before a special judge – a *judex selectus*. The special judge will then hear the evidence and reach a verdict from which an appeal may or may not be allowed. If it is, then the appeal will be argued by lawyers before the Emperor."

"But our situation is somewhere in the middle, isn't it?" said Flaccus. "We had court proceedings and heard evidence in Alexandria, but the trial wasn't over and there hasn't been a verdict."

"In fact," added Proculus, "there really has been no defense case, particularly if several witnesses are coming to Rome and haven't yet been heard from, like Serpentinus and Philogenes. Not to mention those witnesses we think are going to change their testimony."

"So what should be the procedure?" asked Flaccus.

"I'm not sure," replied Severus. "Maybe a *judex selectus* will be appointed to hear the evidence that hasn't yet been presented and to render a verdict. Then an *appellatio* before the Emperor can go forward. On the other hand, the Emperor may wish to interrogate the witnesses himself. That was the preference of the Emperor Hadrian, in his time."

"One thing is clear," added Proculus, "Secundus is the defendant. But who will be the prosecutor. Who is bringing the charges against him?"

"There is no one else but me," replied Severus. "I will have to be the prosecutor."

The next step was to find out whether there would be a special judge assigned to hear the rest of the evidence, or whether the Emperor would prefer to hear the witnesses himself, dispensing with the *judex selectus*. There hadn't been any word of a special judge being selected, but Severus knew if one were chosen, the choice would be made by the head of the Bureau of Judicial Affairs – the *a cognitionibus* – who was also in charge of the Emperor's court. Severus did not know him personally and so could hardly approach him about the matter. But he did know the Urban Prefect, Quintus Junius Rusticus, who had recommended him to the Emperor in the first place to go to Egypt and look into the situation there. Rusticus might know or be able to find out whether there was to be a special judge or not.

Severus therefore sent a long message to the Urban Prefect explaining the situation and asked for a meeting to discuss the procedure that would be followed in Secundus' *appellatio* to the Emperor. Two days later the Urban Prefect agreed to meet Severus to discuss the matter. Rusticus suggested Severus come to his home in the afternoon, two days later. Rusticus said he would be sponsoring a lecture in the auditorium of his home by the Skeptic philosopher Favorinus and Severus was cordially invited to attend and bring friends as well. Their meeting would take place after the talk.

Rusticus added that the lecture would be in Greek and the topic was 'Against the Chaldeans.'

"I suppose," explained Severus to his wife and Alexander, who were dining with him that night, "that Rusticus wants as many people to attend the lecture as possible."

"The topic appears to portend one of Favorinus' attacks on astrology," she answered. "Astrology is what the Chaldeans are famous for, isn't it?"

"Yes," joined in Alexander, "and I want to go to the talk, if I may."

"You both can come. After all, it's a very controversial topic and a lot of people are offended by attacks on astrology. So maybe that's why we were asked to come. Getting people there might be somewhat difficult."

Two days later Severus with Artemisia and Alexander went to the Urban Prefect's *domus*, an urban villa on the Caelian Hill, not far from their *insula* apartment house. They walked and arrived amidst a gathering of litters bearing other guests to the talk. At the entrance, Severus ran into his friend from student days in Athens, Aulus Gellius.

"I'm going to take notes," said Gellius, after exchanging greeting kisses and cordialities with both Severus and Artemisia, "and include this talk in my book."

"Are you still writing *Attic Nights*?" asked Severus. "I remember you starting it when we were students in Athens years ago. I thought you might be finished by now."

"I don't know when I'll ever finish it, really. It's a collection of things I find interesting, and I keep on coming across new things to include. This is just one of them. Anyway, Favorinus is a good friend, and I love hearing him talk and I know already that what he's going to say will be interesting and controversial."

Inside Rusticus greeted the guests, thanked them for coming and had a slave escort them to his auditorium. He told Severus that he had spoken to the Emperor about the procedure for the upcoming *appellatio* and would discuss it with him after the talk.

The set up of the auditorium was similar to other private auditoria for public readings. There was a dais with a chair for the speaker, special armchairs in front for higher ranking guests and benches behind for others in attendance. Severus and Artemisia were shown to armchairs while Alexander was directed to a seat on one of the benches. The room filled up quickly and slaves distributed *libelli* – programs with information about the speaker and his topic.

The programs said Favorinus was from Arles in Gaul and famous for his vast learning and erudition in both Greek and Latin literature and culture. It mentioned he had come to prominence during the reign of Hadrian and recalled a famous quip he had made. When asked why he resisted contradicting a statement by Hadrian when he could have easily have done so, Favorinus said it was foolish to criticize the logic of the master of 30 legions. Eventually, though, he incurred Hadrian's displeasure and was exiled to the island of Chios. However, he was rehabilitated when Antoninus Pius became Emperor and returned to Rome where he wrote, lectured and taught many upper class Romans.

Favorinus came on to the dais dressed in a gray Greek philosopher's mantle. Most striking however was his peculiar appearance. He was an albino with strange white hair and he was a hermaphrodite. People couldn't tell by his looks whether he was male or female and when first seeing him were often shocked or laughed in derision. But at the Urban Prefect's home, fear of offending a powerful host overcame visceral reactions. Everyone kept a straight face, some with difficulty.

Favorinus began with an interesting statement that it was "completely foolish and absurd" to think that just because "the tides of the ocean correspond with the course of the Moon that the Heavens govern who wins a lawsuit about an aqueduct". Much less should we believe that "all human affairs" are governed by the stars and planets. Knowledge about the Heavens was "not at all certain". For instance, there might be more planets than the seven known ones, but men cannot see them because of their "excessive height."

Moreover, the circuits of the heavens take long numbers of years to complete, even ages, so how could anyone know the actual influence of past configurations if it is impossible to observe the repetitions? And different stars are visible from different places on Earth because of its round shape, so people born at the same time must therefore be born under different configurations of the stars and planets depending on their location. So how could their fate be the same?

And how could it be that the fate of people who died at the same time, for instance in an earthquake or the sack of a city, could all have the same fate even though born in different places and at different times under different stellar configurations?

Furthermore, one configuration of the Heavens was present at the time of conception and another at birth, so which one was supposed to foretell the person's character or future?

But, urged Favorinus, it was most intolerable to believe the idea that an individual's beliefs, attractions and aversions, feelings on important or trivial matters, were excited or influenced by the Heavens. Suppose, Favorinus asked, someone wanted to go to the Baths, then changed his mind, then decided to go again, could this ebb and flow be controlled by the planets and stars? If so, men would not be reasoning beings, but a species of "ludicrous and ridiculous puppets".

And, he also asked, if the life and death of men were subject to the Heavens, what about the lives of flies, worms, frogs, gnats and sea urchins? Did they have fates assigned to them by the constellations? Why should the power of the stars be effective with people and ineffective with other animals?

Astrology, he warned, was simply a way for charlatans and sycophants to gain our confidence and take advantage of our credulity for their own profit. Sometimes, he said, they might hit upon something true "by chance or cleverness", but these "are not a thousandth part of the falsehoods which they offer up."

After the talk, Severus met with the Urban Prefect in the library of his *domus*.

"Interesting, wasn't it?" said Rusticus. "Food for thought."

"I agree with everything he said," replied Severus, "and have ever since I was about 4 years old."

"How did that come about?"

"I had an older brother who told me there were no gods and that astrology was nonsense. Since he was 11 at the time, I thought he must know."

Rusticus laughed.

"And when I grew up," continued Severus, "and examined those questions for myself, I found no reason to change my mind. Even if the gods did exist, I would never worship beings whose behavior I would despise in people.

"However, I do admit to being superstitious."

"As are we all," replied Rusticus ruefully. "But tell me how did your 11-year-old brother come to *his* opinion about these matters?"

"I don't know really. Maybe he was precocious. But also he was by nature rebellious. So when our parents and everyone else told him to believe in the gods and things like astrology, he would do the opposite. And when he got older and examined things for himself, as a thoughtful person he found no reason to change his mind."

"Well, I'm a Stoic and believe that *logos* – Reason, pervades the Universe and that we ourselves are endowed with a measure of that Reason. And Favorinus makes reasoned arguments, so we can only hope that his words will encourage people to use their Reason and at least be skeptical."

"I doubt it," replied Severus. "People believe in astrology because they want to, because they think it helps them 'understand' their lives and the world and answers questions that there are no answers to. And I don't think any number of philosophers like Favorinus or logical arguments will change that."

"A gloomy prospect. But probably you're right. Anyway, let me tell you what the Emperor told me about the *appellatio*."

Severus looked at him with renewed interest.

"The Emperor does not want to have a *iudex selectus* appointed to hear the so-called new evidence. He has read the documents you submitted with your report to him, as well as a report sent to him by Secundus' lawyer. He wants to hear and interrogate the witnesses himself. In my opinion he's a very good judge of people. I know some say he's too pedagogical, but really he's a kind and friendly person. He's firm without being stubborn, reserved but not timid and serious but not gloomy."

"You admire him greatly, don't you?"

"Yes, I do. You know he's the Emperor of the world, but he denigrates fame. Can you imagine? A Roman Emperor denigrating fame. He says future fame is really worthless because it depends on a succession of short-lived men with little knowledge even of themselves, let alone of someone who died long ago.

"In any event, Severus, he said he has faith in your integrity and you will not need any *advocatus* to represent you but yourself."

Rusticus gave him a big smile, which Severus happily returned.

On the way home Severus looked at his wife as if to ask what she thought of Favorinus' talk, a look she readily understood.

"You know," she said to him, "Favorinus' talk could make someone skeptical about astrology. But I'm a true skeptic. I'm also skeptical about Favorinus."

XXX

THE PREFECT AND HIS ENTOURAGE ARRIVE IN ROME

Straton was at the docks in Ostia waiting for the arrival of the *Isis* from Alexandria. The ship was already late, overdue by two days. Straton was dressed in an ordinary brown undyed tunic, hardly distinguishable from any number of poor citizens and slaves wearing exactly the same garb. This included the person standing next to him, an undercover agent of the Praetorian Guard named Titus Velleius. He was there for the same reason as Straton, to observe the arrival of the Prefect of Egypt and his entourage. They were, of course, people of interest to Judge Severus, who had sent Straton to observe their coming. But once the Praetorian Guard heard about Claudius Celer's report -- of the criticisms of the Emperors in the letter from the aide of General Avidius Cassius on the Persian front to Secundus in Alexandria -- they became interested in these people as well.

Marcus Aurelius, it turned out, made light of the General calling him a "philosophizing old woman" and Lucius Verus "a freak of extravagance." Aurelius thought it was not a threat nor were the disparaging sentiments unique, as he well knew. In any case, thought the Emperor, the state needed Avidius Cassius right now. He had whipped the eastern legions back into shape and was leading the counterattack against the Persians. The Praetorian Guard, however, was always suspicious of criticism of the emperor they were charged with guarding.

The guardsman Velleius wanted Straton to recognize and point out Calvus' entourage to him when they arrived.

The day was overcast and cloudy, the sea air bracing and the great port humming with activity. It was full of ships of every kind, hundreds of them from almost every land, both commercial and military, from huge superfreighters with more than 10,000 tons capacity to sleek warships. Ships were constantly coming in and going out. Huge derricks – or 'storks', as they were called – lifted cargo on and off decks, while stevedores, both slaves and freemen, were working everywhere. Most were operating in teams and often singing songs as they worked. Clerks were also everywhere, recording everything, every item loaded or off-loaded, keeping the copious records of a record-keeping civilization. But they were doing their jobs silently, without singing, though sometimes with muttering.

Straton and Velleius walked around from the docks to the lighthouse, which Straton remarked was not quite as impressive or as tall as the Pharos Lighthouse at Alexandria, but it was impressive and tall enough.

Velleius swept his arm over the scene and asked with a smile, "What ships are the safest, warships or merchant ships?"

"I don't know."

"The ones in port!"

"Oh," said Straton. "That old joke. So, did you hear the one about the proverbial dope from the town of Abdera who was on a ship that was foundering in stormy weather? His slaves started screaming in fright. Don't worry, said the Abderite. I'm freeing you all in my will."

"Well," countered Velleius, "do you know the one about the Abderite who put a sack of cabbage and onions on the stern of his boat on a calm day? His doctor had told him that cabbage and onions cause wind!"

"Speaking of doctors," replied Straton, "did you hear the one about the man who went to the doctor complaining, doctor, doctor, when I wake up every morning I'm dizzy for half an hour. What should I do? The doctor replied, wake up half an hour later!"

"What about the man with horrible bad breath," countered Velleius, "who went to the doctor saying his tonsils have swollen and dropped. The doctor told him to open his mouth and when he did his breath was so bad that the doctor recoiled in disgust. It's not that your tonsils have fallen, diagnosed the doctor, but your ass has risen!"

"Did you hear the one about the guy who went to the doctor complaining that he was covered in red hot boils and was burning up. Get yourself a kettle of water, advised the doctor, and jump in. You'll have warm water for days!"

"This reminds me," said Straton "of the man at the barber who was asked, how should I cut your hair? In silence!"

"So which joke book have you been reading," asked Velleius. "I have one called *Philogelos* – 'Lover of Laughter'".

"I just remember jokes," replied Straton. "But I'll look for that book."

Suddenly a great commotion rose and people started running to the dock. The superfreighter *Isis* hove into view, its mainmast lowered, but its red topmast still displayed in the manner of the Alexandrian grain fleet. This was the ship that Straton and Velleius were waiting for and they ran toward the dock, but then hung back. Their intention was not to be seen but to see. Velleius also gave a signal to someone waiting in the wings.

"We have a band from the Praetorian Guard waiting to form up and greet the Prefect of Egypt and his entourage. He'll probably be the first off the ship because of his status and position. He'll be easily recognizable by everyone greeting him, of course, but I want you to point out who is who among his entourage. We'll both be following one or the other of them as things progress."

"Is the band here to honor the Prefect?" asked Straton.

Velleius gave a somewhat crooked smile. "More to lull him."

The ship soon docked. It was a beautiful superfreighter. Straton knew its measurements from looking them up at the port authority offices. It was 180 feet long, 45 feet abeam with a hold 44 feet deep, taller than a 4-story apartment house. It had a capacity of 12,000 tons and could carry more than 300 passengers. The *Isis* was painted dark blue with red strakes along the sides. The oars were painted yellow, the golden gilded gooseneck sternpost -- the sign of a merchant ship -- shone as a bright sun emerged from a gap in the clouds, while a statue of the goddess Isis graced the stern.

As predicted, the Prefect and his entourage were first off. The band had formed up but were waiting for Calvus' own family and clients and slaves who had come out from Rome to gather round and greet him first. Straton started pointing out members of the Prefect's entourage, who were behind him and hanging back while the greetings were going on.

"That one with the shaven head in the long white linen robe and palm leaf sandals is Petamon, the Isis priest," said Straton, "while that gorgeous woman with the red hair next to him is Aurora, Calvus' *hetaira* at the orgy and now his concubine. The young man standing next to the Prefect is Secundus. Of the other two standing next to Petamon and Aurora, one must be Serpentinus, his aide, and the other Philogenes, the Homeric scholar and librarian. Both were also at the orgy."

"The tall thin one with the drawn-in face who looks like a snake must be Serpentinus," observed Velleius. "So the other one, the very small one must be Philogenes."

"I agree," said Straton. "So now that we know, I'll follow Philogenes and you can follow Serpentinus."

"All right. And I'll assign the guardsmen with me to follow the others individually. We've all agreed to meet at your judge's chambers in the Forum of Augustus every evening to compare notes. So I'll see you there."

Velleius then walked into the crowd and conferred with other Praetorians dressed non-descriptly, pointing out the people in the Prefect's entourage and making assignments.

The Praetorian Guard band struck up a greeting march and headed toward the Prefect and his entourage, accompanied by coaches, carriages or Tiber river boats ready to transport the arrivals to Rome. Then Straton, Velleius and the other guardsmen all boarded their own waiting coaches or river boats to follow the stream of travelers along the *Via Ostiensis* or the Tiber River into the City.

XXXI

ALEXANDER RECOUNTS HIS MEETING WITH PHILOGENES

Three evenings later, there was a scheduled gathering at Judge Severus' chambers in the Forum of Augustus, as there had been every evening since the arrival of the Prefect. Seated around a citrus wood table were the judge, his assessor Flaccus, police aides Vulso and Straton, his personal secretary Alexander and the Praetorian Tribune Cornelius. The Praetorian guardsmen Velleius was supposed to be there as well, but had not yet arrived.

The table was in the center of the room next to the *scrinium*, a tall circular wooden bureau with cubby-hole shelves for scrolls and files. A white cushioned reading couch was against one wall while official portrait paintings of the two Emperors graced another.

"An interesting day," said Straton beginning his report. "I followed the Homeric scholar Philogenes to the Greek library in the Forum of Trajan, just adjoining our Forum. The same as yesterday, he asked for an old scroll of Book I of Homer's *Iliad* and sat down with it at the same reading table he sat at yesterday. As we planned, Alexander was already there waiting for him. Once again, he started studying the scroll and tearing at his hair." Straton laughed and nodded at Alexander, who took up the report.

"I was seated across the table from Philogenes, and seeing his obvious distress, I casually asked him 'what was the problem?' 'Was he having trouble reading the scroll?' He said, 'How can anyone read this? It must be a thousand-year-old Greek.' 'Close to it,' I said, and told him my name. He said his name was Philogenes and he was from Alexandria. I said, 'I can read it. Do you need some help?' He breathed a sigh of relief. 'Absolutely', he said. 'Can you really help me?'"

"One moment," interrupted Cornelius. "I thought he was *the* Homeric scholar from the Library of Alexandria. How come he couldn't read that old Homeric scroll?"

"Homeric scholar?" said Alexander. "He's an Homeric scholar like I'm a champion gladiator. I even mentioned that this scroll is an old one, not even the standard version of Homer that the scholars at the same Library of Alexandria agreed upon a few hundred years ago. This so-called Homeric scholar expressed surprise. He said, 'really? I didn't know that.'"

"So what's going on?" asked Cornelius.

"He's obviously an imposter," concluded Severus. "They brought him here because he's small the way Philogenes was, maybe even looks like him, and he's preparing himself to pull off an impersonation by learning some things the real Philogenes should know."

"So the real Philogenes *is* probably dead, as Isarion told us," said Vulso.

"I think we can rely on that information now," replied Severus.

"How should we handle this then?" asked Flaccus.

"I think," suggested Severus, "that Alexander should teach him to read Book I of the *Iliad* in this old version for the next few days – he's coming back for help tomorrow isn't he?"

Alexander nodded.

"Good. So make him feel prepared to pull off an impersonation. And then when he appears at the trial to say he saw the slave Ganymede poison the Prefect's cup, he'll be able to read Book I of the *Iliad* to prove he's Philogenes. But then maybe I'll confront him with Book VIII of the *Odyssey* and watch him turn green."

Everyone laughed.

Severus then asked Cornelius for the reports of the other Praetorians following others in the Prefect's entourage as well as Calvus himself.

"The Prefect didn't leave his home at all, though messengers were constantly going out and coming in all day, and people were calling on him, clients and *honestiores*, both Equestrians and Senators, judging from the narrow and broad stripes on their clothing. Some even had magisterial stripes on the hems, so they must be judges or officials like Praetors, Quaestors, Aediles. Maybe even a Consul. In addition, we learned that Calvus is scheduled to meet with Marcus Aurelius on the Palatine tomorrow.

"Secundus also stayed inside, so we don't know what he was doing, but probably he was meeting with the same people his father was meeting with.

"That gorgeous *bacciballum* -- that juicy berry -- the red-headed concubine Aurora visits a local *balneum* every morning for a bath and massage. Then today she was taken on a tour of the City by one of the house slaves.

"Petamon, the Isis priest, is still in the great Temple of Isis next to the Saepta Julia where he went two days ago. As far as we know, of course. It's hard to tell one of those priests from another. They all have their heads shaved and wear the same long white robes and palm leaf sandals.

"And as for Serpentinus, Velleius was following him and he should be here by now to report on today's happenings. He should have been relieved over an hour ago. Anyway, for the last two days, as Velleius reported to us, Serpentinus was looking to find Isarion at 'The Golden Ibis' in the Saepta Julia. We arranged to have the clerk overseeing the store tell him that Isarion is on a short business trip and should be back any day, so Serpentinus should have gone there again today.

"We'll just have to wait a little while longer for Velleius to tell us what happened today," continued Cornelius. "Meanwhile, for tomorrow maybe we can think up a way to approach Aurora. Maybe we can have someone befriend her if she tours the City again and pump her for information. Maybe..."

Just then Severus' court clerk Proculus opened the door to the room and asked Cornelius to come outside. There was a guardsman asking to see him.

"Probably there's word from Velleius," he said, as he walked outside.

He came back without much delay and with a drawn, pallid face.

"It's Velleius," he said. "He's dead. He's been found in an alley with his throat cut."

XXXII

CALVUS MEETS WITH THE EMPEROR AND HIS *CONSILIUM*

The Prefect of Egypt's meeting with the Emperor and his *consilium* of friends and advisors was scheduled for the 4th hour of the morning, after the notorious morning traffic jams in the center of the City would have cleared up to some extent. Any earlier and Calvus' procession from his *domus* on the Esquiline to the Palatine would have become ensnared in the traffic while contributing to the snarl.

Calvus' procession began taking shape even a few hours earlier. The Prefect's clerks and clients, slaves and attendants, as well as musicians, way-clearers and assorted flunkies, had to be organized and arranged before and behind the Prefect's litter, ready when the Prefect came out of his house. When he did, he got into his luxurious 8-bearer litter, the litter was hoisted up and Calvus sprawled casually on the cushions with the curtains only partially drawn so he could see out and wave to the crowds along the route who looked at the procession. Some onlookers viewed the procession with a certain admiration for its splendor, some even waved at it, but some also cursed at its opulence and arrogance and its needless contribution to the traffic jams.

Still, the procession made good time through the center of the City to Old Forum and up the Clivus Victoriae to the Palatine and the Imperial Palace. There Calvus was escorted by waiting attendants to the chambers where the Emperor and his *consilium* had gathered to hear his report on conditions in Egypt. Egypt was in some measure the most important province in the Empire because it supplied most of the grain to the City of Rome. If the flow of grain were interrupted, there would be riots in Rome and the government would answer for it. For the people of the City, as Seneca had warned, were an "immense multitude – discordant, seditious, uncontrollable, ready to run riot and equally endanger itself and others if they broke the yoke."

The *consilium* was composed of some of the Emperor's most trusted friends and advisors. They were all eminent and experienced. Among them were L. Volusius Maecianus, who had also been a member of the *consilium* of the previous Emperor Antoninus Pius. More than that he had been one of Marcus Aurelius' teachers in jurisprudence, a former Prefect of Egypt himself, and the noted author of the definitive 16-volume treatise on Trusts. Also present was Q. Junius Rusticus, the Prefect of the City and Sextus Cornelius Repentinus, one of the two Prefects of the Praetorian Guard, the other being on the Persian front with a detachment of the Guard. Then there was M. Cornelius Fronto, doyen of the Roman bar, and tutor and close friend of both Marcus Aurelius and Lucius Verus from when they were adolescents. Fronto had been a consul some years before and had regularly corresponded with Aurelius for more than 20 years. Also present was Calpurnius Longinus, the *advocatus fisci*, or chief lawyer of the imperial revenue and Q. Cervidius Scaevola, one of the great jurists of the day.

Calvus, for all his self-importance, was intimidated by the overwhelming eminence, experience and intelligence of the *consilium*, almost as much as he was by the Emperor himself. Indeed, Marcus Aurelius was often quoted as saying of his *consilium* that "it is more just that I follow the advice of so many such friends than that my wishes, the wishes of one person, are followed by them."

Calvus reported that conditions in Egypt were good, the harvest and grain supply would be good, and the notoriously fickle Alexandrians would be no trouble. He accounted his time at the helm in Egypt a great success.

After his report, Calvus was escorted into the garden by the Emperor and expressed the hope that the *appellatio* of his son Secundus would be held soon so that he could quickly return to his post in Alexandria.

Then Marcus Aurelius broke the news to him that his successor as Prefect of Egypt was already on route, so time for the *appellatio* was not of the essence. It would be held in due course and Secundus would receive the customary 5-day notice ahead of the trial.

Taken aback, Calvus hardly knew what to say, but managed to ask "why? Why have I been replaced?"

There was no need for Aurelius to mention that he and the *consilium* were unanimous in their decision. There was no point in taking any chances with a Prefect of Egypt whose son was suspiciously in contact with the personal aide to a general in command of legions who was critical of both Emperors. Aurelius said simply, "the *consilium* thought it was time for a change and I agreed with them."

"It's because of that Judge Severus, isn't it? He's poisoned your mind against me. And against Secundus, who he has a grudge against and is persecuting. So I just want to say that whatever report he made to you is false and certainly incomplete because there are witnesses who he never spoke to and others who he intimidated and manipulated to condemn me and my son."

Aurelius listened in silence, but then interrupted to say that since he would be the judge at the trial, his mind has not been made up about the case and he should wait to hear any new evidence in court. With that, he dismissed Calvus and went back into the chamber to confer with his *consilium*.

XXXIII

SERPENTINUS IS HUNTED DOWN

The *insula* apartment building in the Subura was surrounded by personnel of the Praetorian Guard, some in civilian clothes and some in full military dress. It was the 2nd hour of the morning, and the street was already alive with activity. Two agents sat in a taverna across the street from the apartment house drinking wine. One looked like a philosopher -- a long beard, gray Greek philosopher's mantle and walking stick -- the other, in a scruffy tunic, looked like his slave or servant. They were watching one of the 3rd floor shuttered windows and its balcony across the street. Four more agents were playing dice on the sidewalk, clad in ordinary gray or brown tunics, looking like typical idlers of Rome's crowded and lively Subura district. They were stationed beneath that same 3rd floor window. Three more agents stood in line waiting to buy sausages from the cookshop next to the entrance of the *insula*. Two more were on each of the five floors of the apartment building, at the foot of each stairway, keeping the corridors clear. Another two agents were stationed on the roof.

Down the street at the nearest intersection, out of sight of the target *insula*, there was a formation of eight Praetorian guardsmen in full military dress, glittering bronze helmets and armor, with swords drawn and scorpion-emblazoned shields ready. They were waiting for the signal to go. An animated crowd of onlookers and gawkers mingled around them, blocking traffic on the crowded streets. Some were already taking bets on which apartment house or shop the soldiers were going to raid. A number of these bystanders were also Praetorians.

The flood of guardsmen in the area, more than 30 in all, measured their almost paranoid determination. First and foremost was the principle that no one, absolutely no one, kills a member of the Praetorian Guard and gets away with it, no matter how many men or how much time it took. The murder of the Praetorian Velleius, found with his throat slit in an alley, had to be avenged. It was, after all, a simple matter of self-protection, self-defense.

It hadn't taken much investigation to pin the crime on Serpentinus, the creepy aide to the Prefect of Egypt who Velleius had been assigned to follow. Evidently, Serpentinus had spotted Velleius trailing him, lured him into an alley a few streets from the Subura apartment where he was holed up and waylaid him there. It was not known whether Serpentinus even knew who Velleius was. Possibly he thought he was being stalked by a robber or an urban predator of some kind. No one saw the murder, but that didn't matter to the Praetorian Guard. It was not a question of evidence for a law court because who else could it be? The only thing that mattered was that Serpentinus had obviously murdered a Praetorian and he had to pay for it.

Serpentinus was now hopefully trapped inside his apartment on the 3rd floor of the *insula*. It was from there that Velleius had followed him for a few days to Isarion's 'Golden Ibis' shop in the Saepta Julia market and back again. And after the murder, Serpentinus continued what he had been doing, checking up on whether Isarion had returned or not. But he remained under surveillance by Praetorians.

The Praetorian Tribune Cornelius was in charge of directing the raid and making the arrest. He command-ed the operation from the back of a laundry, one of the shops on the ground floor of the target *insula*. Dressed in full battle gear -- helmet, sword, armor -- he munched a Lucanian sausage on a stick and sipped wine, while biding his time.

In the same shop laundry slaves were busy trampling dirty clothes into a large basin of cleansing and disin-fecting urine mixed with fuller's earth. They watched the goings-on with some interest, even if out of the cor-ners of their eyes. Anything was a welcome change from their mind-dulling and smelly jobs.

"What are you waiting for?" asked Vulso who had been invited by Cornelius to watch the arrest as an ob-server. He was also in full battle dress, wearing his transverse side-to-side centurion's helmet crest, instead of a regular front to back crest. He wanted action, not to stand around amid the repulsive smells of a laundry.

Cornelius finished his sausage, sucked on the stick, and gave it to a slave attending him, while wiping off his greasy hands in the slave's hair.

"Now it's time." He gave a signal to an aide who stepped outside and waved to the Praetorians in battle dress. They responded on the double, and with Cornelius and Vulso stepping in front of them, they all charged into the *insula*, past the smelly buckets of residents' feces awaiting collection, and up the stairs to the 3rd floor. Cornelius stopped in front of the door to Serpentinus' apartment and nodded to two burly Praetorians behind him. One had a key obtained from the owner of the building. He stepped forward and as silently as he could inserted the key into the lock, turned it, and pushed fast and hard against the door, which sprang open.

Inside, a nude Serpentinus looked up from the bed in silent, wide-eyed astonishment as the Praetorians rushed in. The naked woman under him screamed. Two guardsmen hauled Serpentinus into an upright, standing position, locked in a firm grip. Another guardsman dragged the woman out of the bed, shoved a tunic from the floor into her hands, and ushered her out the door and down the stairs.

Cornelius drew his military *gladius* and pointed its steel blade -- 20 inches long, 3 inches wide, and double edged -- against Serpentinus' midsection. "For slitting the throat of a member of the Praetorian Guard," he announced to Serpentinus with a grim voice and face.

"I didn't know who he was," Serpentinus managed to gasp out in desperation when he saw the look on the Tribune's face and heard the tenor of his voice. "I didn't know who he was," he repeated pleadingly. "I thought he was a robber."

"It makes no difference," responded Cornelius, looking directly into his eyes. Then, with all his might, he thrust the sword into Serpentinus' stomach, twisted it and pulled it out. Serpentinus made an indecipherable sound somewhere between a grunt, a groan and a scream as blood spurted from his stomach. Then he began to shake and gurgle as a bloody froth came out of his mouth and nose, his life literally "bubbling out", as if to confirm the Latin expression. Then he collapsed, still in the grip of the guardsmen, and died.

"Resisting arrest," announced Cornelius and walked out of the room.

A few hours later Vulso reported to Judge Severus that he needn't worry about Serpentinus testifying at the trial before the Emperor.

XXXIV

ARTEMISIA CONTRIVES TO MEET AURORA AND STRATON SPREADS SOME NEWS

"Why don't I have to worry about Serpentinus?" asked Severus. He was in his chambers, dressed in a white tunic with the narrow reddish-purple Equestrian stripes, arranging documents in the tall circular *scrinium* in the middle of the room.

"Because the Praetorian Guard murdered him," answered Vulso. "I was there."

"I thought they were going to arrest him."

"He was arrested... for about the blink of an eye. Then Cornelius executed him for slitting the throat of a Praetorian, namely Velleius. Cornelius called it resisting arrest, but actually he didn't even have time to resist."

"Does this disturb you at all?"

"Why should it? My own Urban Cohort would do the same, as would the *Vigiles,* as would almost any other police organization whose member was murdered. It's self-defense, deterrence and revenge, all rolled into one."

Severus was tempted to make a few choice criticisms from the points of view of both Roman law and Greek philosophy, but held back in deference to reality. Instead he just shrugged and changed the subject.

"I have some interesting news."

Vulso looked at him inquiringly.

"Calvus is no longer Prefect of Egypt. He's been replaced. I heard it from a reliable source on the Palatine."

"That is interesting. Why was he replaced?"

"That letter from the general's aide on the Persian front to Secundus. It's too suspicious. They would have to be either naïve or negligent to disregard the possibility that Calvus is involved. He may or may not be. But while they need Avidius Cassius to conduct the war, they don't need Calvus to be Prefect of Egypt. It's too risky now."

"Will this be useful to us?"

"I think so. I want to make sure this news gets to certain people – the Isis priest Petamon, for one, and Calvus' concubine, Aurora, for another. I suspect that Calvus brought them both to Rome to lie for Secundus at the trial before the Emperor. If they're bound to Calvus in deference to his position and power as Prefect, as may well be the case, then if he's no longer Prefect, the bonds may loosen or even break."

"But Petamon is holed up in the Isis Temple in the City and Aurora is at Calvus' home. How can we get the news to them?"

"I've been thinking about that. Petamon is easy. I'll send Straton to pose as a follower of Isis as he did in Alexandria and have him visit the main Isis temple here and just spread the news. Since Isis in an Egyptian cult, the news that the Prefect of Egypt has been replaced will be of immediate interest and will spread within the cult.

The priests, including Petamon, will certainly hear about it. They will probably check it out, of course, but since the news is true, they will just confirm it for themselves through their own sources."

"What about Aurora? How will you contrive to let her know?"

"I've been discussing her with Artemisia. My wife has volunteered to try to meet her surreptitiously and see what she can find out. We know from having Aurora followed that she's in the habit of going to an exclusive Roman *balneum* near Calvus' house to bathe every morning. Artemisia's friend Valeria lives nearby, so Artemisia's idea is to stay at Valeria's apartment on the Esquiline for a few days and go to that *balneum*. She can be there for a few mornings before Aurora arrives and try to strike up a conversation with her. Now she can also contrive to tell her the news that Calvus is no longer Prefect of Egypt."

"It's a good idea," said Vulso, "but there's still a flaw. It may be that Calvus is no longer Prefect and therefore not so important a person, but he's still in Rome and still a presence and a powerful one at that."

"You're right about that." Severus mulled it over and then smiled. "Maybe we can have Straton and Artemisia also spread a rumor. I've actually heard it myself from my source on the Palatine, although he may have been joking."

"What's the rumor?"

"That Calvus' next posting will be to Hadrian's Wall in the far north of Britannia and in the middle of winter. We can spread that story. When they hear it, Petamon and Aurora may think twice about tying their futures to someone so out of favor."

Vulso laughed. "Hadrian's Wall is a good place for Calvus. In the middle of winter will also be good time for it. And what's more, it's probably true."

The next morning Artemisia was in the pool at the *balneum* before Aurora arrived. The poolside was elegantly decorated with tasteful mosaics of dolphins cavorting in the sea and the water in the pool was clean and clear enough to see the mosaics of fish at the bottom.

When Aurora came in from the changing room, Artemisia along with everyone else in the pool or by poolside turned and stared. As all bathers, Aurora was nude, but she was more beautiful than anyone else. Her face was stunning, her body lithe. Her hair was naturally red; her head hair straight and long and her pubic hair stylishly arranged into a semi-circular topped triangle. Silent admiration lasted a few moments for most of the women who then returned to their loud and engrossed talking to one another as Aurora entered the water. For others, though, their eyes stayed fastened on Aurora, as did their minds and their libidos.

Artemisia was prepared with a story. Her name would not be Artemisia since she had met the Prefect in Alexandria when she and Severus had had dinner with him, so if Aurora should happen to mention the name Artemisia to him, he might become suspicious. No, she would be Elektra, one of her favorite names, but she would still be from Athens on the principle that convincing liars should stick close to the truth.

Artemisia hadn't yet decided what approach she would make to Aurora. As she was mulling over plausible openings to conversation, she was saved the trouble when Aurora swam up to her and in hesitant Latin asked if she spoke Greek.

"I'm from Athens," replied Artemisia in Greek. "My name is Elektra."

"I'm Aurora, from Alexandria."

"I've been to Alexandria. A beautiful city."

"When were you there?"

"A few years ago," Artemisia lied.

"Are you visiting Rome?"

"No, I've lived here for years." Artemisia began to spin out her made-up story. "Actually my husband and the children live well outside Rome,"-- this to avoid having to invite Aurora to her home -- "but I'm visiting friends who live nearby to do some shopping in the City."

And so the conversation continued quite fluidly between them, as Artemisia and Aurora seemed to hit it off, conversing almost as old friends from the start.

After a while, Aurora said. "Elektra, I don't know anyone in Rome and I need a friend. I feel I can trust you."

"Yes, let's be friends," replied Artemisia, "but first we should get to know each other, right, Aurora?" Artemisia had a pang of feeling bad about herself for her deception. Nevertheless, she continued to play her role. "Come, let's leave here and I'll show you around the City. You can help me do some shopping and I can show you places you might be interested in. We can talk on the way, have lunch at a good taverna, and become acquainted."

"I would love that," replied Aurora.

They left the pool for the changing rooms, passing by the gym where women in scant two piece gym suits were exercising with weights or throwing balls around.

Aurora quickly changed into her simple Greek style tunic and waited outside the dressing room with her slave. Artemisia took more time in donning her more copious Roman stola with the help of two slaves she had brought with her. Her delay was deliberate and when Aurora was out of the room, she told one of her slaves, Galatea, to go on ahead into the center of the City. She was to go into Eunice's shoe store on the Vicus Sandalarius, to Myron's jewelry workshop on the Argiletum and into the nearby "Ostrich and Mullet Taverna". She was to tell the proprietor at each place that when Artemisia came in, they were to recognize her, of course, but to address her only as Elektra. No mention of the name Artemisia was to be made. They should make sure the staff knew to do the same. Then Galatea hurried off.

Artemisia finished dressing and took Aurora by the hand and led her out of the *balneum*. "Let's walk down the Clivus Suburanus to the center of the City. We can go to the Argiletum and to the Vicus Sandalarius. These are some of the most interesting streets in Rome with lots of shops of every variety. Then we'll have lunch at my favorite taverna."

"Sounds wonderful," replied Aurora. "I'm so glad to have met you, Elektra."

"And I you," replied Artemisia. They strolled down the crowded Clivus Suburanus which skirted the Subura. "The Subura," Artemisia told Aurora, "is the City's most vibrant and notorious section. It's teeming with apartment houses mingled with every kind of night life and every kind of shop, restaurant, and place of entertainment you can imagine. The great Caius Julius Caesar once lived here when he was young and the Emperor Nero and his cronies used to come here at night incognito

for a wild time. It caters to all classes, high and low. The
Subura is a hubbub of activity, night and day."

With their slaves trailing behind them, Artemisia
continued to point out various sights of interest, but also
kept up an active personal conversation, which Aurora
was eager to take part in.

"So as we are to be friends," said Artemisia, "tell
me about yourself. What is your life like in Alexandria?
And why are you in Rome?"

"It's not a long story. I was one of six children but
my family was desperately poor and I was very beautiful. I was sold into a house for *hetairai* at the age of 8.
It was an exclusive establishment, it's true, and they paid
my parents a high price for me. I grew up trained in all
the arts necessary to please men. I play the cithara and
flute well. I sing. I dance. I have been taught classics
and can converse with learned men about literature and
philosophy and, of course, I can make love with skill and
faked passion. I made a lot of money for the House of
Selene and was able to buy my freedom with my share
of what I brought in."

Artemisia was both sympathetic and complimentary. Sympathetic about Aurora's fate as a child about
which she could do nothing, and complimentary about
her struggle out of slavery as an adult.

"Yes, I am technically free," continued Aurora, "but
in many ways I am still a slave, a plaything, passed from
one man to another. Right now I am someone's concubine and I don't even like him.

"But what about you, Elektra? Tell me about
yourself."

"I grew up in Athens, as I mentioned. My father
is a professor of philosophy there, a leading Platonist.

He raised me and my brothers and sisters according to Plato's ideas for a Guardian of his ideal State. Since Plato thought there should be female Guardians as well as male Guardians, my father followed Plato's idea that male and female Guardians had to be trained and educated the same way. So I was brought up like a Greek boy, not a Greek girl. I was taught philosophy and other skills and subjects Plato considered necessary, like music and geometry. Therefore I too play the cithara and flute and I'm very knowledgeable about philosophy and literature. My education was aimed not to please men, but to please philosophy, but perhaps it makes no difference. It's the education that counts."

"Perhaps I saw something of that in your face even at the pool," said Aurora. "I think that's why I was drawn to you."

"And I see the same thing in you," Artemisia replied honestly. But now her deception was becoming unpleasant to her because she was beginning to like Aurora as a friend. Maybe, Artemisia thought to herself, she could find a way to help Aurora, rather than betray her.

They had a nice time together, talking, sightseeing, getting to know each other and after lunch went their separate ways for an afternoon siesta. They agreed to meet the next morning at the *balneum* for another day together. Though Aurora had more than once expressed friendship for and trust in Artemisia, she still was somewhat wary of confiding in her, which was, perhaps, only natural in view of the short time they knew each other.

While Artemisia was with Aurora, Straton, dressed in a neat white tunic, was ready to represent himself as a slave working on the Palatine and privy to information, or at least gossip, from the imperial household. He went to the temple of Isis for the morning services. His role as slave in the imperial household was not exactly unfamiliar to Straton. As a child that's exactly what he had been during the reign of Hadrian. He had been freed at Hadrian's death, 27-years ago now, but he remembered that time, mostly with bitterness when he thought about it, which wasn't often.

His task at the temple of Isis was carried out swiftly and successfully. He joined the crowd waiting for the morning dressing and feeding of the statue of the goddess and told the people standing around him in a confidential tone that he had just come from the Palatine and just heard, reliably, that Calvus had been replaced as Prefect of Egypt by someone named Titus Tatianus. And not only was Calvus out as Prefect, but he was also in disgrace and about to be sent to a sort of exile in the north of Britannia for the winter.

His news spread like wildfire from person to person. Straton could even see it spread as the crowd became more animated in a visibly wider circle around him. He also saw someone run up to the priest who was about to officiate at the ceremony and saw the priest listen to what he was being told and his face show surprise. Then the priest turned and ran back behind the curtain separating the crowd from the inner sanctum.

Straton took the opportunity to elbow his way out of the crowd before the ceremony started. He had better things to do than watch any more of what he considered to be superstitious Egyptian drivel.

XXXV

A TRIAL DATE IS SET AND ARTEMISIA MEETS AURORA AGAIN

The next day all parties received the 5-day notice of trial from the Palatine. Announcements of the upcoming *appellatio* would also be placed in the Daily Acts on the newsboards in the Old Forum. This would naturally draw members of the general public to attend in addition to the interested parties and their clients, friends and hangers-on.

Judge Severus and his aides considered the publicity a good sign since the nature of the case, an *honestior* charged with the judicial murder of a slave through incompetence and brutality, would naturally draw the sympathy of the general public toward the victim and turn its antipathy against the accused. But whatever the proclivities of the audience, Severus was preparing to destroy any defense Secundus might make.

The parties were also informed that the trial would be held in a garden on the Palatine Hill. This was not an unusual venue for an imperial court. Emperors were accustomed to hold court wherever they were, both at home and abroad. When in Rome, Emperors not only heard cases on the Palatine itself, but also from Tribunals set up in forums, in parks and gardens and in other public places. This sometimes had unexpected advantages, as when Emperor Claudius, holding court in a forum, was enticed by smells of cooking by priests in a nearby temple, and suspended a trial to join them for lunch. But public appearances were not always so congenial. On another occasion while holding court in the Old Forum Claudius was assailed by an angry mob complaining of rising wheat prices and had to be hustled out of harm's way by the Praetorian Guard.

It was the obligation of all Emperors to dispense justice and salutary for them to do it in public, both for the good of the regime and for them personally. Failure to hear petitions, render justice and make legal rulings would condemn an Emperor in the eyes of the populace. It was his job, as much as defending the country from foreign enemies.

Moreover, court held in private aroused suspicion and resentment. The time Claudius held a secret trial in his bedroom was badly received by Rome's legal community and by the people, when they learned about it. So the regular auditorium at the palace set aside for the imperial court was also open to the public when the Emperor was hearing cases there.

Marcus Aurelius was particularly conscientious about his judicial role and spent what some considered an inordinate time in hearing cases, sometimes even sitting at night or spending extra days in careful consideration of the evidence and legal arguments. He was also noted for his preference for mild penalties and presumptions in favor of the disadvantaged in society, especially minors, orphans and slaves.

The same day, Artemisia and Aurora met again at the *balneum*. They spent the morning together, had lunch and established a growing congeniality, friendship and trust. After lunch they again parted and also agreed to get together the next day. But Artemisia had yet to learn anything relating to the trial from Aurora and time was running out. The trial was only a few days away. As for Aurora, she was both growing closer to Artemisia and becoming more tense. Artemisia was certain the imminence of the trial was preying on her mind.

On the next day, after the *balneum*, Artemisia told Aurora she would take her first to a jewelry workshop where she had to pick up a pendant "they're working on for my daughter." They strolled into the Argiletum, their slaves trailing behind them, and went to Myron's jewelry workshop.

Myron was a wizened old man, bowed over, but vigorous nonetheless. He greeted Artemisia as Elektra, without so much as a grin, and told her the pendant for her daughter was ready. He instructed a slave to bring it out and while waiting took the opportunity to show Artemisia and Aurora his wares. Lapis lazuli, amethyst, jasper, carnelian and various other stones were set out on tables, some for inspection by customers, while others were having designs worked into them by the shop's craftsmen as customers watched.

"Beautiful workmanship," commented Aurora, as she inspected some engraved stones.

"We can make any design you like and engrave stones for rings, necklaces, bracelets, earrings, whatever you want."

Aurora kept on coming back to a beautiful piece of amethyst that was blank, waiting for an engraving.

"Amethysts," said Myron, "are special stones. Not only are they beautiful but they have magical properties, as indeed do almost all stones."

He reached for a scroll on a table behind him. "Do you know Pliny's *Natural History* on the nature of stones? Naturally we keep it on hand. Here, let me tell you what Pliny says about amethysts."

Myron rolled out the scroll to the place he had in mind. "I'll translate it into Greek for you, Aurora. It says that if amethysts are inscribed with the names of the Sun and Moon and are worn hanging from the neck along with baboon hair and swallow feathers they are protection against spells." Both Artemisia and Aurora began to laugh. Myron continued. "However amethysts are used, they will assist people who are about to approach a king as suppliants and they also keep off hail and locusts if used along with special incantations." Both women kept smiling. "I'll grant you," said Myron, "that Pliny notes the same claims are made for emeralds and that he thinks whoever makes these claims must have contempt for the intelligence of men."

"Maybe so," said Aurora. "But if by any chance they help suppliants who approach a king, I would like an amethyst stone as a good luck charm. Do you have something like that?"

"I do," said Myron, with a smile.

Artemisia, knowing that Aurora was in Rome waiting to be a witness at a trial before the Emperor, saw her opening. As they left the jeweler's, Artemisia with her daughter's pendant and Aurora with a small amethyst charm, they headed for lunch at the "Ostrich and Mullet" nearby. When they sat down at a table, Artemisia asked Aurora directly, though seeming to say it half-facetiously, "are you going to be a suppliant before a king?"

Aurora looked distraught. Then she lapsed into silent thought and then seemed to reach a decision. "Elektra, I haven't told you why I'm in Rome, but I will now. I'm here because I'm the concubine of the Prefect of Egypt and his son is going to have a trial before the Emperor. I am to be a witness."

"A witness? But a suppliant is supposed to ask some favor or indulgence from the ruler."

"I may have to be a suppliant and throw myself on the mercy of the Emperor. You see, I'm supposed to testify to what the Prefect and his son want me to say. That I saw something I didn't really see. And I have no choice. I'm a nobody, just an Alexandrian *hetaira*, and they are rich and powerful and Romans. What can I do?"

"The Prefect of Egypt?" said Artemisia slyly. "Do you mean Titus Tatianus?"

"Who is he? I mean Marcus Annius Calvus, the Prefect of Egypt."

"Calvus? But he's no longer Prefect of Egypt. It's all over the City. He's been replaced by Tatianus. Come winter, Calvus is going to be sent to the north of Britannia, almost like being in exile."

Aurora was stunned. "Are you sure?"

"Absolutely. It's all over the City. Everyone is talking about it. I'm sorry Aurora. But your Calvus is in disfavor."

Aurora looked distraught. "What a mess," she said. "What am I supposed to do now? I don't want to testify for Secundus. I certainly don't want to go with Calvus to Britannia. I don't even want to be with him in Rome. I don't even like him. But I'm afraid of him."

"Maybe I can help you," said Artemisia tentatively.

"Thank you, Elektra, but there's nothing you can do. I'm Calvus's concubine, and though I'm not a slave, he has control over me. He has power and influence and I don't know anyone. I'm alone in a strange city."

She held her head in her hands and then looked up. "But on second thought, Elektra, maybe there is something you can do. There just might be someone who can help me. But I don't know where to find him or even if he would help. But he's the only person I know, or at least have met, who is a Roman and is powerful. If only I could find him and throw myself on his mercy."

"Who is this Roman?"

"He won't listen to me, I know. But now I'm desperate. You see, Elektra, when I was in Alexandria there was this Roman judge who came to the House of Selene to question all the *hetairai* who were at a certain party with the Prefect and his son. I thought this person seemed honest and interested in the truth. He found evidence that exonerated a slave who had been falsely accused of a murder and executed."

Artemisia stared almost in disbelief at Aurora, knowing what she was going to say, and who the Roman judge was.

"What's the name of this Roman judge?" asked Artemisia, almost whispering.

"I believe it is Marcus Flavius Severus. And I know he has left Alexandria and possibly he's in Rome. Do you think you can help me find him?"

"I think I can," said Artemisia with a huge smile. "In fact, I know I can."

XXXVI

THE TRIAL BEFORE
THE EMPEROR: DAY 1

The trial commenced at the 3rd hour of the morning. It was another beautiful sunny, warm Italian morning. Birds were chirping and flitting from tree to tree, branch to branch.

A substantial crowd occupied the seats and benches set up in the center of a colonnaded three sided stoa within a garden on the Palatine. There was standing room in the rear and in the stoa itself.

Severus was dressed in his judicial toga, sparkling white with the magistrate's reddish-purple borders, and his law assessor Flaccus and court clerk Proculus were seated next to him at counsel table. The table itself held scrolls and documents neatly arranged for ready reference.

At another table, Secundus was dressed in the black toga of a defendant. Next to him was Calvus, the former Prefect of Egypt, his father by adoption. He was dressed in a bright white toga, the reddish-purple narrow stripe of his Equestrian status on his tunic showing through.

Secundus' lawyer, the same Eggius who had represented him in Alexandria before Severus' court, was with him now at the defendant's table, ready to present the defense case. The table in front of them was also arranged with scrolls and documents. A number of family members and friends, all of the Senatorial and Equestrian Orders as shown by their broad or narrow tunic stripes, sat just behind in a show of support. Some of them, including Calvus, would probably be slated to testify as witnesses to Secundus' wonderful character.

Not to be outdone, Severus also had a number friends and family members of his own seated behind his counsel table. They were there not only to show support but because arguing a case before the Emperor was a special occasion for anyone and family and friends wanted to be there.

Artemisia and the two older children, Aulus and Flavia, were there as was Severus' older brother, the one who had told him as a child that the gods didn't exist. His two children, Severus' nephew and niece, were there too. The nephew was himself a powerful government official in charge of a department in the Bureau of the Treasury. He had been appointed personally by Marcus Aurelius and was a friend of the Emperor's. His wife, also present, was one of the few female reporters for the Daily Acts. Severus' niece was producing her own work of family history and intended to include this trial in it. Also a cousin, who was a highly respected judge in his own right, sat behind Severus, ready to offer him cogent comments and useful advice during the trial.

Water clocks for timing the advocates were set up at the side of the Tribunal. Each advocate, Severus for the prosecution and Eggius for the defense, would be given 6 water clocks -- 2 hours -- to make their opening statements. Also at the side were lictors with bundles of rods, a necessary accompaniment of any magistrate. A statue of Jupiter Fidius, the god of good faith, was set up because its presence was necessary to make an official courtroom.

At the 3rd hour, the Emperor Marcus Aurelius entered the court and took his place on the curule chair set on the 4-foot high Tribunal. He was accompanied by three assessors. They were all members of his *consilium* – the Urban Prefect Rusticus, the Praetorian Prefect Repentinus and the legal scholar and former Prefect of Egypt Volusius Maecianus. They would hear the evidence and arguments of the lawyers along with the Emperor and advise him during deliberations, but the verdict was the Emperor's alone. Marcus Aurelius nodded to a court officer to start the water clock and asked Judge Severus to begin.

Severus stood and addressed the Emperor.

"*Domine*, I am pleased to have this opportunity to address you and your most illustrious and most eminent assessors and to present the evidence in what to my mind, as a judge with many years experience in the courts of Rome, is one of the most egregious cases of judicial negligence, incompetence and malicious brutality that I have ever encountered. The actions of the defendant are a disgrace to the name of Roman law and Roman justice and a clear violation of the *Lex Cornelia* against judicial murder.

"Let me tell you how this crime was discovered."

Severus then began to review the case. He could see he had the attention of the Emperor and his assessors riveted on him. He then recounted how he had been selected by the Emperor to be his emissary and special judge. He was to go to Alexandria to investigate an attempt to assassinate the Prefect of Egypt by poisoning his wine cup at an orgy. The wine cup had dolphins on it and was the personal cup of the Prefect.

Upon arrival, Severus was told that the culprit had already been arrested, tried and executed. It was the Prefect's slave Ganymede, it was alleged, who had committed the crime because he believed that his wife, a former concubine of the Prefect, was still having relations with him.

"Secundus, the defendant here, and at the time the Prefect's stepson, now his adopted son, had been the investigator and judge of the case. He showed me Ganymede's confession and told me it had been obtained under torture."

Severus went to counsel table, picked up a scroll, unrolled it and read it to the court.

"As you hear, the confession alleges that Ganymede obtained the poison from a sorceress named Phna. I asked Secundus whether this Phna had corroborated the confession. I was told, however, that she denied it. *Domine*, as you and your assessors well know, confessions obtained under torture are insufficient by themselves to prove a crime. Roman law requires that they must be corroborated because people being tortured will often say anything to stop the torture. So I inquired further. What corroboration was there? Was there any other evidence against Ganymede? No, I was told. Others had been questioned, but there were no affidavits of anyone to support the confession.

"Why, then, I asked Secundus, had Ganymede been singled out for torture in the first place? Roman law, as we know, requires a specific suspicion of guilt before a lover class *humilior* or even a slave can be tortured. But I was told there was none. Secundus blithely told me he had randomly tortured every slave at the party until someone confessed."

Severus observed the grim looks on the faces of the Emperor and his assessors. He knew he had made his point and went on.

"Obviously then, I had to make my own investigation and so I began to question everyone who was at the orgy. I questioned all the *hetairai* -- and their affidavits and testimony in court in Alexandria are part of the record here -- as well as the guests who were available. I found out that not only had no one seen Ganymede poison the Prefect's cup, but that Ganymede had never left his position behind one of the dining couches which was nowhere near the Prefect's table. This is also confirmed by other slaves who served at the party and who testified in Alexandria. It became clear, indeed certain, that Ganymede could not have physically put poison in the Prefect's cup. Therefore, he must be innocent.

"But why then had Ganymede confessed?" Severus paused to take a drink of water from his table and allow the question to sink in. "I questioned the *quaestionarius*. As his affidavit and testimony in court in Alexandria detail, the defendant Secundus ordered the torture to be increased until it was so unbearable that Ganymede confessed in order to stop it. The torturer himself said that afterwards he had nightmares about what he was ordered to do.

"The slave Ganymede was then tried by Secundus as judge, found guilty by Secundus and sentenced to death by Secundus. Secundus even told me with perverted pride that he allowed Ganymede to be beheaded, the death penalty for an upper class *honestior*, rather than be crucified or thrown to the wild beasts as a lower class *humilior* or slave."

Severus then went on to recount the unavailability of witnesses he wanted to talk to; Ganymede's wife; people at the party like Isarion; Philogenes and Serpentinus. And then Pudens' assistant Celer. "Were these road-blocks to investigation deliberate attempts to curtail a full inquiry?" he asked rhetorically.

And then Severus told about the finding of the phony and incomplete affidavit being worked on in Secundus' apartment, supposedly from the missing Philogenes. And of Secundus' foisting of the phony document in court in Alexandria.

"This deceit demonstrates a guilty mind."

Then Severus concluded.

"Normally a prosecutor at this point will face a de-fendant, point a finger directly at him and accuse him of being guilty. But in this case, I cannot even bear to look at the defendant's face. As a Roman judge myself, I find few crimes more disgusting than judicial murder."

With that Severus sat down.

The Emperor looked to the defendant's table and nodded toward Eggius, the defendant's counsel. He took up his position before the Tribunal and began.

"*Domine*, the eminent prosecutor has made a case which sounds compelling but is in fact woefully incom-plete. He questioned whom he could, it is true, but he did not question all the possible witnesses. He did not question people at the party who were not available to him at the time. Specifically, the antique dealer Isarion, the Prefect's aide Serpentinus and most importantly the great Homeric scholar from the Library of Alexandria, Philogenes. In addition, the questioning of those he did talk to, like the Isis priest Petamon and the *hetaira* Aurora, was intimidating, suggestive and overbearing. The prosecutor alleges that Secundus manipulated the investigation to produce a conviction of the person he thought had done it. But the prosecutor himself has manipulated the questioning of the witnesses to produce the result he wanted. Namely the conviction of Secundus. I don't know the reason for the prosecutor's animus; I don't know why he got it into his head that Secundus committed judicial murder. But he himself has committed a judicial crime. Not murder perhaps. But a skewing of the facts to try to exonerate a person who was guilty, namely the slave Ganymede, and skewering of a fellow Roman judge, namely Secundus."

Eggius then went on in this vein for another hour, using up his time in a personal attack on Severus and a whitewashing of Secundus.

When his sixth water clock ran out, the Emperor called a recess for the day.

"I trust, Eggius," said the Emperor doubtfully, "that you can supply us with witnesses who will back up your claims tomorrow."

Marcus Aurelius and his assessors then left the Tribunal and court was adjourned for the day.

XXXVII

THE TRIAL BEFORE
THE EMPEROR: DAY 2

Instead of his usual breakfast of white bread soaked in milk and honey, for the second day in a row Severus had a bowl of ground wheat cereal with honey, the breakfast of the Roman legions. It was fortifying for the court battle ahead.

He and Flaccus, who had stayed overnight at Severus' apartment to discuss the case, then left at the 1st hour for the second day of trial, walking down the Caelian Hill, past the Flavian Amphitheater, into the Old Forum and up the Palatine Hill. The morning weather was somewhat brisk, so they both wore *paenula* coats over their togas, though with the hoods lying back on the coats.

"They're following the standard strategy of lawyers in a trial," explained Severus to his assessor. "If the facts are against you, argue the law; if the law is against you, argue the facts; if both are against you, smear your opponent."

"Who do you think they'll call as witnesses today? The false Philogenes? Petamon? We know they can't call Aurora now."

Flaccus said the last name with a conspiratorial smile. Three days before, after Aurora asked Artemisia to find Judge Severus for her, Artemisia did just that and immediately took Aurora to see Severus in his chambers in the Forum of Augustus. They discussed her predicament and decided on a plan, which had been carried out the day before the trial started. As decided, Aurora went as usual to the *balneum* to meet Artemisia and once again they walked into the City. But this time they ditched the slave escorting Aurora by conveniently getting "lost" in the crowd. Aurora was then met by Straton and taken to a safe apartment in the City. Once there, she sent a message to Calvus saying she would not lie for him or for Secundus and she was never coming back. Calvus and Secundus and Eggius were just too busy preparing for the trial to do anything about it.

"As for Petamon," said Severus, "we'll just have to see. We know Straton successfully planted the information about Calvus' dismissal at the Isis temple. I don't think Petamon will now be so anxious to lie for Calvus at a trial.

"My feeling is they will rely on Philogenes. They don't know we've discovered he's an imposter. I hope they call on him."

"Have you decided how to handle it if he's called?"

"I think so. We'll see how it plays out."

The court session got under way in the same place as the day before. By the 3rd hour the sun was out, the air was warming up and the garden was cheerful. The same large crowd as the day before had already gathered, filling the seats and benches in the audience and the standing room behind. Severus' friends and family were once again seated behind his table.

Severus noticed that a small, nervous looking man, who fit Alexander's description of the false Philogenes, was seated just behind the defense table with Secundus, Calvus and Eggius.

The Emperor called the court to order and nodded to Eggius to begin.

"*Domine.* Yesterday the prosecutor told the court about the difficulty he had in Alexandria in finding witnesses he wanted to talk to and blamed their absence on the machinations of the defendant.

"Today I must inform the court that the defense is encountering the same problem in Rome. Our witnesses are disappearing. For instance, the attendees of the Prefect's party in Alexandria. We knew the antique dealer Isarion was in Rome, but now we are told by his business associates that he is unavailable, on a business trip in Sicily. He is a purveyor of Egyptian antiquities. Why has he gone to Sicily for Egyptian antiquities?

"Then the Isis priest Petamon. He came with us from Alexandria to Rome and then went to stay at the main Isis temple in the City. When we went there to bring him to this trial as our witness, we were told he is unavailable. The Isis cult says he is on a mission for them somewhere. They won't even say where.

"Then there is Serpentinus. We understand from people at the *insula* where he was staying that he was killed by the Praetorian Guard some days ago."

The Praetorian Prefect serving as one of the assessor's on the Tribunal leaned over and whispered into the

Emperor's ear. Eggius halted his narrative while this was happening.

"I understand," said Aurelius, "that he murdered a member of the Praetorian Guard and was killed resisting arrest."

"So it is alleged," shot back Eggius. "We don't know the full story. But whatever it is, he is another witness that would have aided the defense.

"And just the other day, the day before this trial, another of our witnesses, Aurora, who also was at the party in Alexandria and came here to testify, went missing. A message, allegedly from her, said she won't be back. So something strange is happening to our witnesses in Rome, just like what we are told happened to the prosecution witnesses in Alexandria. Severus blamed Secundus for what happened there, implying that Secundus tampered with his witnesses. I leave the implications of what is happening here and who is to blame for tampering with our witnesses unspoken. This court can draw its own conclusions." Eggius paused to take a drink of water from his table and let the implication sink in. Then he continued.

"Fortunately, whoever contrived to sabotage the defense and arranged for our witnesses to disappear was unable to make a thorough job of it. For the most important witness for the defense is here and will testify right now. He is the famous Homeric scholar Philogenes. He will swear an oath before this Tribunal and testify that he saw Ganymede slip a powder into the dolphin cup at the party. His testimony will show beyond a doubt that it was Ganymede who put poison in the Prefect's cup. And if Ganymede is guilty, Secundus must be innocent!

"I call Philogenes to the Tribunal."

A small man dressed in an immaculate Greek tunic rose from behind the defense table and approached the Tribunal.

Severus rose.

"Normally I would ask the Tribunal to have this witness take an oath, but I don't want him to violate any oath. The reason is that I know this witness is not Philogenes, the Homeric scholar who attended the Prefect's orgy. He is an imposter. And I can prove it."

"This is an outrage," shouted Eggius in anger as he rose from the defense table. "An outrage!"

"Yes," replied Severus. "It is an outrage. But perpetrated by the defense. *Domine*, this witness was discovered at the Library of Trajan taking out scrolls of old versions of Homer's *Iliad*, trying to read them in preparation for his imposture at this trial. He was unable to cope with the ancient Greek and a former librarian had to teach him how to read Book I of the *Iliad* in its original ancient Greek. He is prepared for that. But that is all he can do.

"I ask this court to question him on any other book of Homer, ask him technical questions on Homer's writing, for instance, on the differences between the language of Homer in the *Iliad* and the *Odyssey* or ask him any other questions concerning Homeric scholarship. I guarantee he will not be able to answer. Because he is no more an Homeric scholar than any of us is a charioteer in the Circus."

"Is this true?" asked the Emperor of the witness. "Are you really not Philogenes but an imposter?"

"I, I, I..." said the witness, and then turned to look at Secundus and Calvus.

"Don't look at the defendant," said the Emperor. "Look at me. And tell me about the difference in Homer's language between the *Iliad* and the *Odyssey*."

"I don't know. I'm too nervous to think."

"Then tell me who at the Library of Alexandria made the critical edition of Homer that we use today?"

"Callimachus," blurted out the witness, taking a stab with the name of a famous librarian.

"Surely a Homeric scholar should know, as even I do, that it was Aristarchus of Samothrace and Zenodotus of Ephesus."

One of the assessors leaned over and said something to the Emperor, who smiled and asked, "then answer something simple. What is contained in Book XXV of the *Iliad*?"

"Book XXV? The Trojan horse."

"There is no Book XXV," said Aurelius. "Book XXIV is the final book. So whoever you are, you better tell me the truth. If you do, I may pardon you. If not…"

The courtroom was in pandemonium, the crowd animatedly commenting to each other about what was going on.

The witness flung himself on the ground, arms spread forward in supplication. "Oh great Emperor, great living god, great son of a god, great pharaoh, I throw myself on your mercy."

"Pick him up," said Aurelius to a lictor, who put down his bundle of rods and picked up the witness.

"I am not a god," said the Emperor. "This is Rome. Here the Emperor is just a man. After he dies he can become a god if the Senate votes to make him one. As of now, however, I'm still a mere mortal.

"But I want to know what your real name is and who put you up to this imposture."

"Oh great god, my name is Demetrius. They said I looked like this Philogenes. I never met Philogenes. They said I could be him. No one would know. I could prepare a little in a library. They gave me money."

"Demetrius, who gave you money?"

"He did. He turned to face the defense table. Secundus did it. He paid me in gold."

The Emperor motioned to a lictor to move Demetrius away.

"Secundus to the Tribunal," commanded Aurelius.

At the defense table, Eggius and Calvus buried their heads in their hands. Most of their friends and clients in the seats behind them looked this way and that in distraction; the others glared at the backs of the three in front.

Secundus in his black toga, his head bowed, slowly stood up and slowly shuffled toward the Tribunal.

"What do you have to say for yourself?"

Secundus straightened up and his voice even sounded a note of defiance. "I needed a witness, someone to tell the truth that Ganymede did it. I know Ganymede did it. I couldn't find anyone because Severus was against me and intimidated all the witnesses. No one would speak up for me. So I procured this Demetrius to tell the truth, that's all."

"The trial is over," declared the Emperor. "There is no need for any deliberations. Secundus, I find you guilty of judicial murder under the Lex Cornelia.

"Because you are an Equestrian, an *honestior*, the highest punishment under the law for this crime is exile. I therefore sentence you to exile on an island."

The audience couldn't contain itself and burst into applause and cheers.

Secundus couldn't accept what was happening. "If Ganymede didn't poison the Prefect's cup, then who did?" He shouted in distress and anger. "Who did?"

"That's not the issue," said Aurelius mildly. "The issue is that you as a judge procured false evidence and condemned an innocent man to death."

Several lictors then half-dragged Secundus out of the court. "Who did?" Secundus kept shouting. "Who did?"

Severus stood up and approached the Tribunal before Aurelius had a chance to end the proceedings.

"*Domine*," he addressed the Emperor, "despite Secundus' guilt and disgrace, the question he was asking – who *did* put the poison in the Prefect's cup? – is still a good one and remains to be answered."

"Yes," replied the Emperor, "I can see that. But how are we to know now? Do you know?"

"Yes, *domine*, I do. Or at least I can make a compelling case for what happened. But it will take a while and I would ask for Secundus to be brought back to court to hear it."

"Very well," replied the Emperor. "We will convene again tomorrow morning at the 3rd hour to hear the question answered – who put the poison in the Prefect's cup?"

XXXVIII

BEFORE THE EMPEROR: DAY 3

The proceedings on the third day were not held in the garden on the Palatine. Instead, after Severus had sent a message to the Emperor that information might be revealed that could be considered a State secret, Aurelius decided that the Tribunal should be set up in a courtroom inside the *Aula Regia*, the Imperial Palace. He reasoned that since the trial of Secundus had technically ended with a verdict of guilt for judicial murder, what was to follow would be an investigative hearing. It was therefore neither necessary nor desirable to hold the proceedings in public.

The Tribunal convened promptly at the 3rd hour. Marcus Aurelius and his assessors occupied the front of the courtroom, along with the lictors and the statue of Jupiter Fidius. Severus and Flaccus sat at one table facing the Tribunal and Calvus, Secundus and Eggius sat at another.

At the Emperor's nod, Severus rose and began.

"*Domine*, initially we have to solve the question of who the poison in the Prefect's cup was intended for.

The Prefect Calvus? Or the person who actually died, the Imperial Post inspector Pudens?

"Ostensibly the poison was meant for the Prefect. It was in his cup, after all. But, if so, who put it there? And why? Who among the people at the orgy had a motive to kill the Prefect? It was here that we ran into a serious problem. As Calvus himself said in no uncertain terms, none of the guests had any motive to kill him. On the contrary, each had good reason to want him to live. Each was profiting off their relationship with him.

"Here I want to stop to point out something important about the guests at the Prefect's orgy. With the exception of Pudens, and the *hetairai*, every guest was engaged in a criminal enterprise! Let me say that again. Every guest was engaged in crime!

"The librarian Philogenes was stealing books from the Great Library. The antiques dealer Isarion was producing and selling fake antiques and distributing stolen books. The Isis priest Petamon was involved in the distribution of the stolen books and fake antiquities through his Isis temple. Serpentinus, the man who later gratuitously and expertly killed one of our Praetorians and killed the real Philogenes as well, seems to have been a professional assassin. And Secundus, who, *domine*, you have already found guilty of judicial murder, was then engaged in overseeing this criminal gang and all its crimes.

"But what about the Calvus? What was his role, if any? Was he unaware of what was going on under his nose? Was he an innocent dupe of Secundus? Or was he a knowing participant in all of it? Maybe even the actual ringleader. I will leave that question for the moment but it must remain in the air while I discuss some issues relevant to it."

Severus paused for some water. Then he continued.

"First, why was Pudens a guest at this party? He had nothing to do with any of the other people there. Calvus told me that Pudens was a last minute substitution because a guest – a sub-Prefect – was called away and couldn't be there. Since Pudens happened to be making a report to the Prefect when he learned the sub-Prefect couldn't make it, he decided on the spur of the moment to invite Pudens to honor him for all his years of honest and dedicated service to three Prefects.

"Honor him? By introducing him into the midst of a gang of criminals? By inviting him to attend an orgy with these thieves and murderers? What kind of honor is that? We even learned from the woman paired with Pudens at the orgy that he was appalled by the nature of the revelries. I ask, how much more appalled would he have been if he had known the nature of his fellow guests and what they were up to? I answer. He would have felt totally dishonored. Not honored."

The faces of the Emperor and the assessors were visibly starting to harden, their glances at the Calvus becoming sidelong and openly hostile. Severus noticed it and continued.

"So what was Pudens doing there? What really caused Calvus to invite him and insert him into the midst of that gang of criminals? We know from the Prefect that Pudens had just made a report to him. Calvus told me it was about something trivial. Too trivial to even remember what it was. But I am skeptical. Why? Because Pudens had just discovered something worthy of reporting to the Prefect. I mean, of course, the letter intercepted from the aide of General Avidius Cassius on the Persian frontier to Secundus, the letter criticizing the two Emperors in a rather snide and subversive way. I needn't mention the exact words, *domine*, because you know them. And I'm sure Secundus and Calvus know them as well."

"Yes," said Aurelius. "I know them. And to me they don't seem very terrible. I've been called much worse that a 'philosophizing old woman' and Lucius Verus much worse than a 'freak of extravagance'."

"Yes, *domine*, to you they might not seem serious. And probably to Pudens they didn't seem all that serious either. Which is why he might feel safe in reporting them to the Prefect, perhaps with the idea that the Prefect would warn Secundus to back off before things became serious. If Pudens thought otherwise he likely would not have tipped off a conspirator that he was onto the conspiracy.

"But I would suggest, *domine*, that Pudens' death proves that he was sadly mistaken. I would suggest that Calvus and Secundus knew that the criticisms of the Emperors in that letter were not mere jests or mild criticisms. Quite the contrary. I would suggest they knew perfectly well that there was a real plot developing to overthrow the Emperors and that they were part of it. And so because Pudens had stumbled onto it, he had to be silenced. And that is why Pudens was invited to the orgy. Not to be honored. But to be murdered."

Both Calvus and Secundus were visibly shifting in their chairs. Calvus started to rise to say something, but the Emperor's glare was enough to make him sit back down. Aurelius and the assessors were glued to the speaker.

Severus continued.

"Now we have a motive to kill Pudens. And as for opportunity? The Prefect clearly had the best opportunity to put poison in his own cup. Of course, he could have asked Secundus or his personal assassin Serpentinus to do it. But why complicate matters? Nothing would have been simpler for Calvus than to do it himself. To put poison in his own cup and then exchange it with Pudens' cup or to slide his cup close to Pudens or even put it into his hands when, after sex and with his eyes averted or closed, Pudens reached behind for a drink.

"And how do we know that Calvus is a party to all this? How do we know that Secundus didn't do it all by himself, while Calvus remained in the dark, merely a dupe of his stepson?

"Two good reasons. One. The Prefect knew that Secundus was engaged in crime in Alexandria because I told him so when I was there. I told him about the stolen book ring and about the fake antiques and about Secundus' complicity in these crimes, if not direction of them. And, of course, the Prefect was aware as well of the charges of judicial murder against Secundus. And yet, *domine*, and yet, despite this knowledge Calvus went ahead with the adoption. He didn't disown his stepson or even postpone adopting him as his son. He went ahead as if nothing had changed. To my mind, this is a virtual endorsement of Secundus' crimes.

"But there is an even stronger reason. And it is this. Calvus certainly knew the real Philogenes, the real Homeric scholar who he sometimes had as a guest at his parties -- to impress people, Calvus once told me. Therefore, he knew that the person who was posing as Philogenes, who came to Rome with him as a member of his entourage, was an imposter. He knew all along that the person foisted on the court as the real Philogenes was a fake. And yet Calvus sat there while a fraud was being

perpetrated on the Imperial court itself, on you personally *domine* and on your assessors. Calvus sat there and
said nothing. Why would he do that unless he was party
to the whole scheme himself?

"So I would suggest that far from being a dupe or a
person in the dark, that Calvus betrayed the Emperors
from the start and directed all the schemes – the fake
antiques, the stolen books, the conspiracy against the
Emperors and the murder of Pudens, which he himself
carried out. And, by the same token, he is a conspirator
in the judicial murder of his slave Ganymede for a crime
he himself had committed. Calvus put poison in his own
cup and saw to it that Pudens drank it!"

Aurelius motioned for Severus to sit down. He
turned to Calvus and motioned for him to stand up.

"I don't know," said the Emperor, "exactly how much
of this is true, but it seems much of it must be. And I feel
personally betrayed by you because you certainly knew
the false Philogenes from the real one and said nothing.
You allowed a fraud to be perpetrated on me. You may
have an explanation or not. And I will give you an opportunity to reply when you wish. Not now, of course,
because this is not a trial today, just an inquiry. But there
will have to be a public trial. You can respond then in as
great detail as you like."

Aurelius paused and looked straight into Calvus's
eyes.

"Or, I might suggest, you can consider an alternative
because a public trial will inevitably involve a certain
amount of sensation, if not disgrace, whatever the result.
And the alternative I am suggesting is the road to complete freedom recommended by Seneca."

With that, Aurelius stood and left the courtroom. For everyone understood exactly what he meant. Because everyone knew perfectly well the famous road to freedom recommended by Seneca.

It was 'any vein in your body.'

EPILOGUE

MARCUS FLAVIUS SEVERUS:
TO HIMSELF

A few nights later we all celebrated the end of the trial with a big banquet in our *triclinium*. I reclined on the head couch with Artemisia, while Flaccus and Proculus shared another and Vulso, Straton and Alexander reclined on a third. Our two guests, Aurora and the Praetorian Tribune Cornelius, shared another couch and seemed quite taken with each other from the start. Our slaves Glycon and Galatea shared another couch. Our three children also joined us, though they sat upright at their own table.

The food was excellent, from eggs to apples, with tender and delicious ostrich meat as the main course. The wine was a very old and outstanding Setinian sent over as a gift from the palace, a wine we or anyone else rarely can get nowadays. It was one of two gifts I received that day from the Emperor. The other was a very rare and old scroll of Book I of the *Iliad*. I passed it around to everyone to admire and then displayed it on a table.

Sometime during the dessert a messenger arrived from the palace. I opened the tablet, started to read it, and announced to everyone:

"Calvus has taken Seneca's advice."

Aurora made an audible sound of relief and rested her head on Cornelius' shoulder. Cornelius shot one arm and fist into the air in triumph and put the other arm protectively around Aurora.

"Which vein did he open?" asked Vulso with a little laugh.

"He had a team of doctors open four of them. Both wrists and the veins at the back of his feet as well. He then went into a hot bath in a steam room and after a time silently passed away."

"Did he leave a departing message? Was there anything relevant in his will?" asked Artemisia. I read further.

"It doesn't say. But his suicide speaks volumes."

Aurora interrupted. "I want to say something now."

Everyone looked at her.

She looked at Severus. "Artemisia has told me how you figured out that Calvus poisoned his own cup and got Pudens to drink it, but that you left vague how this was done. I know how."

Aurora stopped for a drink of wine and to gather herself together.

"I know how it was done because I did it. Calvus told me he was playing a joke on Pudens and told me to switch cups, to move Pudens' cup out of the way and put Calvus' cup just within Pudens' reach and to do it while no one was looking. I picked a moment when Secundus was dancing on the table, when people were throwing grapes, when Pudens was distracted by his *hetaira*. Then

I switched the cups. After Pudens drank it and died, I didn't know what to do, but Calvus said I had saved his life, that the poison was meant for him. He ordered me to keep quiet about the switch. He said it was just a joke that went wrong. I didn't really believe him, just like I didn't really believe Ganymede had anything to do with it. But who was I to tell? How could I say anything? I was afraid I had done something wrong. I was afraid of Calvus. But now that Calvus is dead, now I can speak."

She buried her head in her hands and began to sob. Cornelius moved to comfort her.

"Under Roman law, you're not responsible," I told Aurora. "You had no intent to commit a crime. You had no knowledge of what was in the dolphin cup. You innocently did what the Prefect told you to do. Calvus is the guilty party, not you."

"Why did he do it?" asked Artemisia. "Calvus had reached a pinnacle of success as Prefect of Egypt. Why did he have to turn it into a criminal enterprise? Why did he have to plot against the Emperor? Why did he betray the Emperor's trust?"

"Corruption is an old – if dishonorable – tradition," I replied. "Even Seneca, the great philosopher, feathered his nest at the court of Nero. What did his critics say about him? 'By what wisdom, by which precepts of philosophy had Seneca acquired 300 million sesterces during four years of imperial friendship?' And how many others have there been in our history or the history of any other country.

"So Calvus is not unusual. Corruption is endemic. So is a lust for power. So is crime. Aristotle says poverty is the cause of crime. I know that Marcus Aurelius feels that crime is basically caused because people are ignorant of what is right and what is wrong, of what philosophy calls 'The Good'. He says that if people understood, they would not commit crimes. But they don't really understand. They are presented by life and society with temptations and delusions that steer them into false paths. As an Emperor and a philosopher Marcus Aurelius tries to pursue 'The Good', but must inevitably be betrayed by those who don't."

"You haven't betrayed him," said Artemisia.

I appreciated her saying that. "For a time I felt that I was betraying him. After all, I was sent to Egypt by Marcus Aurelius to protect the Prefect. Instead I brought him down. Is that not some sort of betrayal?"

"Hardly," said three people at once. Vulso finished the thought. "You brought a corrupt Prefect to justice. You brought a murderer to justice. That's not betraying the Emperor. That's carrying out his wishes."

"I suppose it is," I replied. We all looked at the gift of the *Iliad* scroll displayed on the table and at the bottle of rare wine sent over by Marcus Aurelius. "I suppose it is."

HISTORICAL NOTE AND ILLUSTRATIONS

A s an historical note, the real name of the Prefect of Egypt at the time of this story is not Marcus Annius Calvus, but Marcus Annius Syriacus. Since nothing is known about Syriacus' character, it should stay that way.

Most of the words and sentiments of Marcus Aurelius expressed by him and said about him in this book are from his writings, either the Meditations, his letters to Cornelius Fronto or as recorded in the Augustan Histories, i.e. *Scriptores Historiae Augustae* (SHA).

The letter of General Avidius Cassius criticizing the Emperors and Marcus Aurelius' response to it are based on actual reports in the Augustan Histories, SHA *Avid. Cass*. I.8-II, though of a later date than here. In 175 CE, 12 years after the events in this book, Avidius Cassius staged an unsuccessful revolt to overthrow Marcus Aurelius.

Aulus Gellius and Favorinus were historical persons and Favorinus' lecture in chapter XXIX is recorded by Aulus Gellius in his *Attic Nights*, III. 1.

Other historical personages mentioned in the book are Q. Junius Rusticus, who was the Urban Prefect at the time, and the members of Marcus Aurelius' *consilium* and his assessors at trial.

The jokes exchanged between Straton and Velleius in chapter XXX are from the ancient joke book, *Philogelos* – Lover of Laughter. The surviving material is from the 4th century CE, but there are references to joke books as early as the 2nd century BCE.

The superfreighter *Isis* described in chapter XXX was an actual ship of the Alexandrian grain fleet.

Translations from the Latin and Greek are my own.

The fresco on the cover is from the Villa Boscoreale near Pompeii.

The bust of Marcus Aurelius and the illustrations of Ancient Alexandria and Ancient Rome are accessible on multiple web sites through Google Images.

The illustration of the Prefect's orgy is by Ruth Chevion, whose careful editing, insightful suggestions and personal and loving support contributed substantially to this book.

Made in the USA
Middletown, DE
25 February 2022